S0-AWX-936

"The eagles," Glamiss, ever practical, prompted. "Are they under any control?"

"Partially. Sometimes."

Glamiss made an impatient gesture. "What sort of answer is that, Vulk?"

"I cannot tell you, Warleader. The adept is weak. I think perhaps it is a child. But there is other danger. Beyond the valley—near it—above—an old man—" The words became slurred and jumbled as they often did when the Vulk's strange mind left its body.

Emeric seized the thin shoulders and shook Asa sharply. "A warlock? Are the rumors true, Asa?"

"Leave him," Glamiss said shortly. "He will be useless for a bit. Let him rest. And no more about a damned warlock. This is a punitive expedition for Ulm—not a hunt for sinners, Emeric."

A sudden scream, high-pitched and furious, froze the priest and warman where they stood . . .

Ace Science Fiction Books by Robert Cham Gilman

THE WARLOCK OF RHADA

coming soon:
THE REBEL OF RHADA
THE NAVIGATOR OF RHADA
THE STARKAHN OF RHADA

ROBERT CHAM GILMAN

THE
WARLOCK OF RHADA

ACE SCIENCE FICTION BOOKS
NEW YORK

THE WARLOCK OF RHADA

An Ace Science Fiction Book / published by arrangement with
the author

PRINTING HISTORY
Ace Science Fiction edition / October 1985

For information address: The Berkley Publishing Group,
200 Madison Avenue, New York, New York 10016.

ISBN: 0-441-87310-3

Ace Science Fiction Books are published by
The Berkley Publishing Group,
200 Madison Avenue, New York, New York 10016.
PRINTED IN THE UNITED STATES OF AMERICA

Chapter One

Of his youth in the last of the Dark Time, St. Emeric of Rhada wrote: "I suspected, but did not know with certainty, that Glamiss was born to conquer. We rode together on Ulm of Vara-Vyka's business as simple arms-brothers, and we spoke of God in the Star, and of politics, of course. Have I not said we were young? And do the young not feel sure they know what is best for all men? But it was The Warlock of Rhada who taught us the long reach of Destiny."

This reference to a "Warlock of Rhada" in Ulm's fief on Vyka, parsecs from Rhada, has puzzled scholars for almost thirty centuries. It appears in St. Emeric's *Commentaries*, written when the great Navigator was a very old man. Who was this Warlock who taught saint- and conqueror-to-be about the "long reach of Destiny?" We do not know. Early chroniclers tell us that Emeric, by birth a Rhadan noble, struggled all his life against "the sin of arrogance and pride." We know that his presence on Vyka, and his position as military chaplain to the warband of Ulm of Vara was a punishment for some infraction of the Way. The Grand Master Talvas Hu Chien had removed Emeric from command of his

1

starship and—the phrase is still used among Navigators—had "put him on horseback" to teach him humility.

In the fall of the Standard Year 3946 GE (the exact date is uncertain) Nav Emeric accompanied Warleader Glamiss (a bonded mercenary at that time, though Vykan by birth) on a punitive expedition of some kind into the Varangian Mountains (the name dates from a later period—in 3946 the mountains were uncharted). It was there, apparently, they encountered the mysterious Warlock—and having done so, went forth from that place to change the history of man in the galaxy.

> —Nav (Bishop) Julianus Mullerium
> *The Life of St. Emeric,* Middle
> Second Stellar Empire period

In that Dark Age men imagined that the Great Sky was but a thousand kilometers above them. The crumbled remnants of the First Empire lay scattered like dust across the galaxy. Unity was a concept unknown. There was only the Order of Navigators, the worship of God in the Star, and a million bandit chieftains on a thousand worlds of wilderness. There was little history and less law. The warmen ruled by the strength of their arms and the sharpness of their iron.

Such was Glamiss's time.

> —Vulk Varinius (Academician of the Council
> of Ministers, 625-870 New Galactic Era),
> *The Vykan Galactons,* Middle Confederate
> period

The troop had been traveling since dawn: fifty warmen, a Vulk, and a priest Navigator. For a dozen kilometers they had followed the river coursing down from the unknown mountains, but for the last hour they had angled away from the tumbling water, traversing the rocky slope toward the crest of the ridge that formed the last natural obstacle between them and the valley of Trama-Vyka. The horses, all war mares, grumbled as they padded over granite and shale; the warmen were silent, for they were Glamiss's men and well-disciplined. Harnesses jingled softly and the harsh light of the Vyka sun shone through the feathery conifers and dappled the steep hillside.

The troopers were armed in the manner of the Vara-Vykans, dressed in shirts of chain mail, their legs booted or wrapped in weyr skin buskirs, swords slung across their backs with the hilt at the left shoulder. The Varan pennons hung limply from their lances in the still mountain air; the white sunlight was hot on their furred and surcoated shoulders.

When the two lead riders reached the crest of the ridge, the warleader raised his hand to signal a halt. "There it is," he said to the cowled and mailed priest-Navigator at his side.

At their feet the rebel valley stretched away in rising terraces toward the northern mountains, white with snow and the melting glaciers. A cool breeze rose from the land below and ruffled the fur edging on the warleader's cape. The mares muttered to one another in their guttural Rhadan dialect and clawed at the rocky ground.

Emeric Aulus Kevin Kiersson-Rhad, priest and Father of the Holy Order of Navigators, eased himself in the saddle and studied the valley of Trama. It did not look damned, yet it well might be. The Order had heard tales of warlockry in the rebel valley. Emeric was here, armed with all the awesome spiritual powers of the Holy Inquisition. The red fist sewn on the cowl of his habit proclaimed it. Behind that crude symbol stood all the righteous powers of the Order: a thousand starships and the moral sanction of the Grand Master himself. Once Glamiss's small troop established itself within the valley, Emeric the Navigator would hold the power of life or painful death over all its inhabitants.

It was a beautiful valley, Emeric thought. Not the sort of place where one would expect to find sin and abominations. Nearby, the slope fell steeply away into a talus of silvery gray rocks and fleshy brush, green leaves veined with amber. Several hundred feet below the talus, whose face gleamed with quartz and metal ores, the forest of tall and feathery conifers began once more, and beyond that the river, its course gentler here, twisted and curved gracefully through broad and fertile meadows of mountain grasses.

But dotting the meadows Emeric could see bare trees, their woven branches reaching high into the cool air, and in the highest branches, great eagles nested. He murmured an Ave Stella. He had heard dark stories of the eagles of Trama. Their armored heads glinted in the sunlight, and from time to time one would spread its wide pinions and cry out. At this distance the shrieks were faint, but they had an almost human quality that raised the hackles on the back of the priest's neck, for it was said the animals of the valley of Trama were bewitched, that they contained the damned souls of some of the most wicked of the Old People.

Even as he watched, some of the great birds took flight. The light of the Vyka sun glittered on the talons, on the tips of the wings, and on the outthrust feet. Emeric's mare, a roan called Sea Wind, danced beneath him, baring her teeth and stretching her own fighting talons at the sight of the rising birds.

Glamiss said, "Can there really be weyr flocks enough here to feed both the warband *and* those eagles?"

It was the withholding of weyr-tribute that brought Lord Ulm's warmen into the valley. To withhold what was due the lord was rebellion and must be punished.

The first year that the Tramans did not send their tribute, Ulm had been too busy elsewhere to take action against them. The second year the Order of Navigators became involved. Local priests had heard rumors of witchcraft in the valley and had reported it to the Bishop. And now, finally, three years after the first act of defiance by the weyr-herders of Trama, here was a column of Lord Ulm's warmen *and* a priest-Navigator to represent the Holy Inquisition.

To carry the Red Fist of the Inquisition into a relatively harmless village of herdsmen was not an assignment pleasing to a highborn lord Nav, a descendant of princes. But like it or not, Emeric Aulus Kiersson-Rhad, priest and pilot of the Order of Navigators, had orders to investigate Trama for warlockry, witchcraft, or for any evidence of worship of the two Adversaries, Sin and Cyb. If he discovered these abominations, he was empowered by the Grand Master of Navigators to burn miscreants and blasphemers.

The religious mission was a punishment, Emeric realized. His ecclesiastical superiors thought him too ready to question, too proud of his birth, too ambitious to wait for advancement in the Order's good time.

"Whatever there is in this valley, there will be less when we pick it clean for Ulm and the Inquisition," Emeric said heavily.

Glamiss gave him an amused look and said ironically, "That isn't the remark of a starborn lord and priest, Emeric. What will become of us poor mercenaries if the nobility starts developing a conscience?"

There was always a slight edge between them. Emeric was, indeed, starborn—the cousin of Rhadan kings. Glamiss, on the other hand, was a common man, a mercenary, dependent for his future on his sword arm.

Glamiss said, less ironically, "I was born in a village not unlike this one, Emeric. We were cold, poor, and hungry. We were lucky if we saw a priest once in three years. If folk slip into the worship of devils, of Sin and Cyb, can you blame them?"

Emeric studied his friend soberly. "It is for asking questions like that that I am here, Glamiss, on horseback, instead of piloting my own starship through the Great Sky. Men manage to create their own devils no matter where they are, or how isolated."

"Or so the Order tells us," the warman murmured.

Emeric made the sign of the Star. "The evidence is all around us. The dead places, the ruins no one can approach because of the wasting death. Men grew too grand, too filled with self-love—and Sin and Cyb destroyed them. That is enough for men to believe."

"Spoken like a true priest," Glamiss said coldly. "*Men* destroyed the Empire, Emeric. Not devils."

"My point precisely, Glamiss Warleader. What we call Sin and Cyb, the Adversaries, men once called Satan or Asmodeus or Nergal, or a thousand other lost names. But at bottom it was always man himself who brought down the wrath of the Star or God or Jehovah—"

Glamiss asked impatiently, "Did the men of the Empire know magic?"

Emeric raised his eyes, shaded, to the yellow star. "There is the Vyka sun, Glamiss. If it didn't rise tomorrow, would that be magic? Sin and Cyb at work? Or would it simply be that some process was taking place that you, a man, did not understand? Magic begins where human knowledge leaves off. The line between the known and the unsuspected is different for every man in every time. *Faith,* on the other hand, is something quite different. Men live and die, learn and forget. But there is a God in the stars and He made the heavens. There is a psalm: *'The heavens declare the glory of God; and the firmament showeth his handiwork.'* That is all. Men who understand that know that there is no 'magic.' Not of the sort you mean."

"Science, then," Glamiss pursued, using the forbidden word.

The priest signed himself. "It is now the will of God in the Star that men be kept from the temptations of science, Glamiss Warleader. It is best that they leave the old knowledge to the Order of Navigators who will share it in good time. Remember that Sin and Cyb are the Adversaries. They wait— always. If I have failed to convince you of this it is because I am a poor priest. I know my failings, friend. I am noble and consequently tend to be arrogant. I question too much. That is why I am here, a horseback chaplain, instead of doing God's truest work as a pilot of starships." He fell silent, sick with longing to be again on the bridge of a starcraft, a holy proof of God's power and mercy, preserved by His goodness from the holocaust and entrusted to His holy Navigators.

Glamiss said, "Don't misunderstand me, Nav Emeric. I have no desire to feel the fires of the Inquisition. As for the people of this valley, they are rebels. In Vara's name, I'll make them pay for that. But will you—in *God's* name—deliver them to the stake if it turns out that they have stumbled onto bits of the old knowledge?"

"The Order Militant decides, not I alone," Emeric said. "If there is Sin and Cyb in Trama, the sinners will receive the mercy of Talvas."

At the mention of Talvas Hu Chien, Grand Master of all Navigators, even Glamiss made the sign of the Star. The terrifying old man held the lonely worlds of the Great Sky in a grip of fear and awe. He was Prime Inquisitor as well as Grand Master, the spiritual vicar of all men, Controller of Starships, Scourge of Warlocks and Witches, of Cyb and Sin. Under Talvas, the Order had become the Order Militant. A scattered priesthood of men who piloted starships had become the supranational church of all the lands that once comprised the provinces of the Empire.

Emeric thought of the great, shadowed bays of the starships he had traveled in: vaulted and groined ceilings lost in the darkness overhead, men and horses jammed into the humming metal chambers surrounded by flickering torches and the smell of war. Emeric, as a Navigator, had known the open bridges of the holy craft. He had seen the mysteries of the shifting stars, the glory of open space—the Great Sky. The starships had been built by the men of the Empire. They were eternal, almost as holy as the Stars themselves. In a universe where such things could exist, there could probably be magic, as well, and a need for inquisitors.

He raised his eyes to the ice-bound mountains rising above the valley. One heard rumors in Vara that there were unholy things in those mountains, and that this was the reason the simple people of Trama had failed to send their tribute to the lord of their lands. Even the troopers murmured and listened to the rumors of a warlock—*The* Warlock—who had poisoned the hearts of the weyrherds of Trama against their rightful lord.

Ulm of Vara-Vyka was little better than a brute: a stinking animal of a man. But he was lord of these lands and it was the duty of his captains to enforce his rights and privileges. As a warleader of the Vykan warband, Glamiss would perform his duty. No more, no less. Rebels to the flail and sword. Still, Glamiss could remember his own beginnings, and it was a bitter thing to savage poor people one understood so well.

He crossed his arms over his dagger and flail and squinted speculatively at the westering Vyka sun. Half the day was gone; it would be night before the troop could reach the floor of the valley and build a fortified camp. It would be better, perhaps, to bivouac here on the ridge and test the valley people tomorrow. Besides, there was something threatening about the eagles of Trama, something more than the memory of rumors of magically controlled animals. If the birds were truly bewitched and chose to defend the valley, he would have to go carefully. It would not do to be defeated now. Glamiss was a young man with ambitions, and his plans did not include a check at the hands of peasants and ensorcelled birds.

He called to a trooper, who stumbled across the rough ground with the ill-temper of the habitually mounted man. Glamiss instructed that a camp be built and that the game, killed earlier in the lower valleys, be butchered and divided among the war mares.

When the warman had gone he turned again to the valley and the mountains beyond, trying to sense their mystery. In a short time he would call the Vulk to him and use his powers, and he would discuss his plans with Emeric, who was a gallant warman as well as a priest. But for the moment his thoughts were his own and he would keep them so.

For some reason he could not fully fathom, he felt on the edge of a great change in his life. He would not always be a mercenary captain for men such as Ulm, the lord of Vara. In some way that he did not understand, yet with complete certainty, he knew that one day he would rule his own lands. That was an absurd thought for a penniless soldier, yet he was convinced of it. The moment would somehow come and he would seize it. Men followed him willingly, and yet that was not the reason for his certainty. It was something deeper, more instinctive. *Mystical*, Emeric called it. Glamiss smiled to himself. The noble Rhad sensed it and, being more a man of intellect than was Glamiss, perhaps understood it better. "You are a born ruler, Glamiss," he had once said. "What a pity you have no country."

And Glamiss had then almost told his friend of the dream—that dream he had had since childhood, of himself standing astride an island between two broad rivers, with hundreds of starships in the sky and a glittering host behind him. He had a starred crown on his head, a feathered cloak on his shoulders, and a flail and dagger of gold in his hands. What a fantasy that was, he thought, yet how *right* it seemed. And what a sour disappointment to wake in the cold stone barracks and see the pale, distant stars shining through the unglazed windows on a bleak and primitive land nearly empty under the dark sky.

Where were the armies? Where the feathered regalia of a star king? Where the armada of starships?

It will come, he thought. *It will come.*

And if the destruction of the valley of Trama and its people was one small part of the cost, he would pay it. Regretfully, but he would pay it.

Chapter Two

The Rhadan warlock Cavour (Early Second Empire period) once suggested that starships could attain velocities in excess of 200,000 kilometers per standard hour. Not only did he run the fatal risk of the displeasure of the Order of Navigators by these calculations (in an earlier age he would have been burned), but he earned the derision of his contemporaries. His computations, based on the known elapsed time for flight between the Rimworlds and Earth, resulted in a hypothetical diameter for the galaxy of 12,800,000 kilometers. Even Cavour, a learned man for his day, was shaken by this immense figure, and recanted.

Interregnal investigators, such few as there were, believed that a figure of 666,666 kilometers represented the exact diameter of what they called "The Great Sky."

> —Matthias ben Mullerium, *The History of the Rhadan Republic,* Late Second Stellar Empire period

—and for the treatment of certain as-yet-unconquered diseases, cryonic storage offers the best hope. It is not too fantastic to imagine a man of the future, suffering from cancer, leukemia, or some other illness, spending ten, twenty, or even a thousand years in low-temperature suspended animation waiting for medical science to solve his particular problem. It is even possible that atomic-powered, fully automated facilities could awaken a given patient when the computer in charge decided that sufficient time had elapsed, or when further cold-storage might irreparably damage the patient's tissues. What a magnificent awakening! To open one's eyes and see the World of the Future! Great, teeming, clean cities; vistas of—

> —Dawn Age fragment discovered at Tel-Manhat, Earth, in the Late Second Stellar Empire period

The Warlock, so-called by the ignorant folk, stood on the ferroconcrete tunnel-mouth of the hospital and stared with blind eyes at the valley of Trama. He was facing south, across the lower couloir of the unnamed glacier that had, for two thousand years, gradually receded, leaving a pebbled moraine and a half dozen icy, leaping rivulets that plunged into the valley to feed the more slowly moving river.

He could not remember clearly when he had come to the hospital. The weather had been warmer then, and the glacier had been high above the entrance to the deep caverns and halls and wards. He was almost certain that the hospital had been completely alive, thronged with star-class patients. Cyborgs had been everywhere, attending to the last needs of the soon-to-be Sleepers. His memories were indistinct because drugs did damage the brain, and so did the Sleep, if it lasted too long. And no one knew exactly *how* long was *too* long. No matter. He had been blinded by trilaudid and on the way to death when Dihanna insisted that he take the Sleep.

Dihanna! The name evoked a surge of emotion, a terrible longing, a thrill of pleasure. He remembered sailing his goldenwing—a spaceship made like a jewel and driven by the pressure of light on golden foil sails a thousand meters tall— with Dihanna by his side. He saw again the Jovian moons in the dark sky and heard the sound of Dihanna singing and playing the synchromion so that the ghostly melodies filled the fragile hull with the music of the spheres.

How beautiful was Dihanna—the Right Honorable Lady Dihanna alt Aldrin, royal cousin of the Rigellian Emperor, Patroness of the lands of High Canopus, Mistress of Vega—even now, her titles rolled easily off his tongue and, Great Star!, he could not remember his own name—*could not remember his own name.*

Tears formed in his blind eye sockets.

How long had he been here?

The glacier—it had moved from the place he remembered in the high ravine, and it had at some time covered the entire slope of the mountain down to far below the present tree-line. It had left the moraine as evidence. And then it had receded, and the feathery conifers had grown again, and the cyborgs had left the hospital, and the folk of the plain had lived and died and had been driven, generations ago, back into these meadowed valleys. The bulky instrument implanted in his left shoulder hummed and whispered and translated the light and shadow of Vyka's day into impulses his brain could accept as sight. It "saw" the weyr herds grazing, the thin smoke rising from the peasant hovels near the river.

These people knew almost nothing of the Empire, of the Rigellian Galactons, of the provinces and cities and worlds without number that he (whom they called the Warlock) knew.

So long, then?

Time enough for the very galaxy to change, to become empty, for a civilization of peasants and herdsmen in animal skins to take over.

He frowned, trying to remember. There had been civil war on the Rim when he took his leave of Dihanna. And racial troubles in her lands of High Canopus. She had said, "I will wait a year. If they cannot give you back your eyes, I will join you and wait with you in Sleep." Yes, he was almost certain she had said that. He *remembered* it; they had been standing on the great promenade of the Starship *Delos*, surrounded by the thronging, brilliantly dressed passengers for the Outer Provinces, and the orchestra had been playing and below,

Nyor, Queen City of the Stars, a blanket of gems in the velvet night of Earth—

"Earth," he said aloud, grieving. *"Earth, Dihanna—"*

The memories (or were they fantasies of a sick mind?) drifted. Dihanna had never come. No one had come to wake him. His entourage had been a glittering multitude, and now they were all gone. There was only the silent hospital and the tranquil valley and the vast emptiness of this world of mountains and forests and distant plains.

Dihanna is dead. Dihanna is dust. Somehow, he *knew* that was true. Great Star, the *time* that must have passed! For he was old.

He knew that the cold Sleep did not kill. It slowed the body processes almost to the point of cessation. A man might sleep for two hundred years and age no more than a few days. Yet he was old. He could see the old man's hands when he held them before the lenses of his "eye"—the skin dry and fusty, the veins blue and knotted, the fingers frail and twisted. He had been a young man when he boarded the *Delos,* a prince. The Patroness of High Canopus, a cousin of the Rigellian ruler of the Empire, would know no other sort of man—

Yet, had she finally known one? A civil war in the Rimworlds was a small thing in an Empire of a hundred thousand star systems. Yet *had* Dihanna—and all those other glittering folk of Nyor—in the end known some dark barbarian soldier, an atom-blast in his hand, scything down the ancient order of things?

Oh, Dihanna—yes, she was dead. Nyor was dust. There was no Empire. There were only the mountains and the simple folk of the valley they called Trama, the empty sky and the alien star standing now near the zenith of a pale and greenish sky.

He stirred and his metal-mesh hospital gown rustled. The gown fed him, warmed him, probably protected him, as well. He had not yet had cause to know. For lack of anything better to do he had trained the wild eagles of the valley to hunt for the valley folk who, disgustingly, ate meat—red and bloody. For a half-year, through a change in the season, he had roamed the hospital. At first, he had searched for other Sleepers. Then he had called for a cyborg to come and serve him. But there were neither Sleepers nor cyborgs. And there was a fine dust on the gleaming floors, the dust of millennia, his sick mind told him. Somehow, he had been missed or left behind when the hospital had been evacuated—*how long ago?* And why? Had the civil war they had discounted so laughingly that night on the decks of the great *Delos* come plunging through this place with all its barbarian horror? He thought not. There was no destruction. The library was intact. The pile continued to supply power and light and heat. No, the medics and the cyborgs and the Sleepers had gone away. In some haste, he saw signs of that. Those civilized doctors and those magnificently made cyborgs had fled in panic from whatever savagery had descended on the complacent, corrupt, and glittering Empire that had lasted—in his own time—for five thousand years.

The folk of the valley, who sometimes worshiped him as a god, sang the chants of their dark past. The Warls, they called them: the prayers concocted by witches and warlocks to protect them from the fury their ancestors remembered. In the grieving laments and sagas of racial memory lay the dark tale of an Empire (a Golden Age, they said—well, it was not quite that) shattered, collapsing, sinking to barbarism.

> *From the rage of the star-raiders,*
> *Save us!*
> *From the fire in the sky,*
> *Protect us, O Warlocks!*

And now the snow had come and gone three times, and he still remained in the abandoned hospital, not knowing what else to do. He queried the computer, but the machine knew nothing of time. He radio-searched the hyperlight commo bands, and there was no human sound. If the great starships still flew, as the primitive folk of Trama claimed they did, they were mute. Whoever piloted the ships understood their systems poorly, if at all.

Often, the suspicion that nowhere in all the galaxy was there anyone like him left alive drove him to the brink of lunacy and suicide. But he lived on, for he had been a brave man and courage remained.

He would have occasional fits of kindness toward the dull

folk of the valley. Like a mad Prometheus, he would give them useful knowledge: the mill in the valley was his innovation, he cured sick children capriciously, ranted history and Imperial protocol into their frightened faces. He taught the youngest daughter of the village chief to tame the eagles when he found she had a gift for the mental disciplines. He remembered, vaguely, lessons in mind-touch from the eyeless race of Vulk—but when and where and, always, how long ago? In a great palace, he thought, in some dark place where a single great moon lit the night, shimmering like silver on the tide of two great, placid rivers. A thousand years ago? Two thousand? Ten?

A short time ago, the hetman and the elders had climbed the moraine, bringing sacrifices of horrible red meat, performing unspeakable rituals. The lord of the nation in which the valley lay, they said, would soon send soldiers to punish them for withholding tribute, and they begged for help. They were like the lower classes always, the Warlock thought disdainfully, unwilling to fulfill their obligations to those set above them. (Had he heard that plaint before? He seemed to listen to an echo of similar words spoken in a great hall by a supercilious man seated on the Star Throne. Was it someone called Rigell? Was it the Galacton? But the Galacton was dust—as Dihanna was dust. The memory vanished like mist in cold sunlight.)

The skin-wearing savages of the valley disgusted him. He sent them away. What could a blind old lunatic who imagined he belonged in another time do if armed men came into these mountains? What did he *want* to do? The hetman did not speak of civilized men, but of barbarians in armor. He felt bleak and abandoned. Dihanna had not come as she promised. No, she had met instead men in steel corselets and armed with the starlight—a thousand years ago, ten thousand years ago—

A dark hatred rose in him like a bilious tide. His old hands trembled with rage. Let them come into the valley at their peril. There were instruments in the hospital, instruments meant as healing tools, but he would be less than a man of the Empire if he could not transform such things into weapons to terrify and destroy barbarians.

With his eye humming and clicking as it changed focus, he

turned and walked back into the dimness of the tunnel beneath the mountain. The drug-hunger was upon him, and he shuffled swiftly toward his sleep-tank, feeling the preliminary gentle probing of the million microscopic needles in his living, silvery robe.

Chapter Three

—of the various diversions available to travelers in
the Province of Vega. Certain of the eagles of Aldrin
have been bred as receptors, and thus the adept may,
with mental amplification, *become* one of Aldrin's
eagles for a time, hunting and actually shedding blood.
"Eagle-riding" is fast becoming a popular sport among
the wealthiest of our Rigellian nobles.

Aldrin's other inducement, of course, is the widely
known Cryonic Suspension Center, where presently in-
curably ill patients may await—

> —Golden Age fragment discovered at Aurora,
> Middle Second Stellar Empire period

With my companion Warman Oelric of the Foragers,
I was riding on the northern bank of the Foaming River
at a distance of some fifteen kilometers from my Lord
Ulm's Black Keep on the river delta, and it came to pass
in that time and place that we were attacked by three
great birds. Of weight they were more than one hundred
kilos each, and of span, fully eight meters, and each
pinion was armed with great claws as were their feet. It
was these birds, in the service of Sin and Cyb, who mur-

dered my companion Oelric of the Foragers, and not I,
as God in the Star is my witness.

> —From the Vykan Archive, a statement made
> by an unknown warman of the garrison on
> the Archery Field, where he was put to
> death. Late Interregnal or Early Second
> Stellar Empire period

Shana, the daughter of Shevil Lar the hetman, known as
Shana the Dark, crouched on her haunches and watched the
savage birds who had formed a circle around her. She had
been repeatedly warned by the Warlock and by her father to
avoid disturbing any convocation of the eagles, and in truth
the creatures were in a savage mood at this moment, billing
one another and eyeing the girl with eyes of metallic rancor.
But with the pride of the adept, she had climbed the cliff to the
aerie when she saw the birds gathering, certain that they would
tolerate her presence. Now she was not so sure: the cruel bird
thoughts plucked and snatched at her human brain angrily.
She had never known the birds to be so hostile, even in their
time of molt.

The master bird spread his wings and screeched defiance
first at the invaders of the valley, then at the weyrherds in the
meadows below, and finally at Shana. Though the words were
not in any sense human, he was saying that Shana was as much
an intruder as the strangers and that the flock must now return
to its ancient ways. "You cannot any longer compel us. We
will kill as we choose." The alien thoughts tumbled through
Shana's mind in a sickening torrent of the blood of weyr and
the torn flesh of men. Shana shivered, and one of the birds
nearest her in the convocation circle struck at her with his
razor-sharp bill, opening a small cut on her naked arm. She
reacted instantly, striking back, her small fist banging feebly
against the eagle's armored throat. But with the blow she
hurled the mental key, the simple thought-pattern taught her
by the Warlock, that could inflict pain on the birds. All in the
circled squawked and danced, and the individual against
whom Shana had loosed the discipline gagged and gasped and
struggled for balance. Instantly, the birds nearest him began

to strike at him until his iridescent feathers were spattered with brownish blood.

"Stop," Shana said. "Enough."

The circle subsided into guttural angry cluckings and squawkings. The lidless, non-human eyes fixed themselves on the girl with such coldness that she gathered her skin skirt over her thighs and shivered. But she persisted. "I am the Falconer," she said aloud, repeating the ancient ritual the terrifying old man in the mountain had taught to her. "You have been bred to obey me."

This was untrue. The birds were native to this place. They had been here long before Shana's people came to the valley. But the Warlock said that these were the magical phrases, and that the birds learned the ritual as nestlings, and even before. It was part of something he called their "genetic code," and when an adept such as Shana said them, the birds *must* listen and obey. "To do otherwise would be like a man willing his heart to stop beating," he had said.

But Shana's control was not as firm as she had imagined down in the safety of the valley. Up here on the cliff it seemed to her that the vicious creatures might break free of her domination at any moment. She was bitterly afraid and sorry that she had been so brash as to intrude herself into the convocation of eagles.

She said, "Who are the strangers?"

The birds fluttered and danced and said that they did not know. Nor did they care, Shana knew. They were men. And they were men not covered by the taboo she, with the Warlock's help, had put upon the eagles against killing the men of Trama. Yet she suspected that if the eagles began by attacking the strangers, who must be Lord Ulm's soldiers, they would end by breaking the prohibition and savaging the people of the valley and their flocks of helpless, grass-eating weyr.

Shana could not imagine a slaughter of men, for she was sixteen seasons old and had never seen men killed. But as a weyrherd, she could visualize the slaughtered flocks and this was real to her: real and terrifying.

The hot sunlight of Vyka burned down on the bone-littered rock shelf where the aerie overlooked a patch of meadow and a bend in the river. Shana was sweating. She wiped her damp

palms on her small breasts and closed her eyes, trying to see
through the eyes of the eagles. The birds' thought patterns
were frightening and chaotic; the Warlock had explained to
her (impatiently, testily) that they only seemed so because they
were not human. Through the clutter of images came a bird-
memory of the strangers, seen from high above. A line of shining men. Armor, Shana thought, *as the eagles see it*. Well,
there was no doubt that the intruders were warmen; the village
elders had been expecting them, this full season past. But there
was a brown man with the soldiers, brown with loose, coarse
skin. *The habit of a priest-Navigator,* Shana thought with sudden panic. She and the folk of the valley feared the clergy and
the Red Fist of the Inquisition even more than they feared the
Adversaries, Sin and Cyb.

Her fear confused the mental discipline and she lost the
images. Her mind retreated through the cacophony of blood
and hunger and shrieking cries that customarily filled the tiny
minds of the great birds. As she mentally fled, she recognized
the eagles' resentment of her—the puny human creature who
forced them to hunt only outside the confines of their valley.

She came to her knees and bits of bone and rock cut into her
naked shins. She straightened so that she knelt among the
great birds, her eyes on a level with theirs. Suddenly she raised
her arms, hands spread, in a grotesque parody of a bird taking
flight. She gave them the command: *"Go! Fly! Keep watch!"*

The convocation erupted into angry screaming, for the
eagles had no wish to obey her, but she was the adept and they
unwillingly stretched, stirring the bones and dry leaves and
twigs that littered the rock as their great clawed pinions beat
the air and they lifted from the aerie to soar on the currents
rising along the cliff from the valley below. The rock-face
seemed to erupt with birds and their shrill cries echoed across
the meadows and the river.

Trembling, her breath coming in short, shallow gasps,
Shana stumbled down the narrow ledges toward the land
below. There was blood on her brown arms and legs and her
bare feet burned on the hot rocks, but she did not pause as she
ran to give the folk warning of the thing the eagles had seen.
And as she ran, her adept's mind felt still another thing, a
strong pulse of mental power coming at her from the southern

ridge. She reviewed the eagle-images and became aware of a thing she had missed on first probing. One of the tiny men rode with the Lord Ulm's warmen. She did not know what this might mean, but the strong brain-waves were upsetting the birds, setting their cramped minds at odds and making them behave irrationally.

Her fear grew stronger and her naked feet burned on the sun-heated rocks. Shevil would know what must be done. She ran on, dark hair streaming and thick terror in her heart.

Chapter Four

Fear the Vulk, for he sees without eyes and knows the Black Arts and dreams of the blood of children. He is not as men are.

—From *The Vulk Protocols,* authorship unknown, Interregnal period

How little we really know of the Vulk. We believe that he lives long, that he touches minds, that he loves men. We do not know *how* long, or if he really knows *our* thoughts, or *why* he should love us. Of this alone we are certain: in ten thousand years of star-voyaging, only the Vulk have we found sharing our eternity.

—Matthias ben Mullerium, *Vulkish Customs Among the Rhad,* Late Second Stellar Empire period

Glamiss could hear his troopers behind him making camp. The scent of the freshly killed game was heavy in the clean mountain air. He dismounted and shouted for the Vulk to be sent to him, then returned to his moody scrutiny of the valley. The eagles were flying again. Something had disturbed them and sent them soaring away from their steep cliffs and bare trees.

The war mares danced and stretched their claws and Glamiss said dourly to Emeric that he had better dismount before Sea Wind's nervousness unseated him.

The priest's mare and his own, Blue Star, were gifts from Emeric's cousin, Aaron, a young man already known as Aaron the Devil, who was heir to the lands of the Northern Rhad and the conqueror of the Central Rhad's plains and grasslands. If Rhada were ever to have a single ruler, that ruler would surely be Aaron.

Glamiss bit his lower lip in gloomy thought. All across the galaxy the warlords were stirring, each in his own land, with great ambitions. The worlds of the Great Sky were thinly peopled. Planetary populations numbered in the hundreds of thousands—though the exact figures were unknown. It had not always been so. In the time of the Empire, the legends told of billions upon unnumbered billions. The priests claimed that Sin and Cyb destroyed the Golden Age. Glamiss suspected that it was something more mundane: war first, then pestilence, then war again, with star-destroying missiles, and finally a great aeons-long night of barbarism. But now there was a tension in the galaxy. Men on horseback were trying to re-create a world that men like gods could not preserve. *And what shall my part in it be,* Glamiss wondered? *What hope for the dream?* He was more than twenty seasons old and he ruled nothing but a warband that did not even owe him allegiance, but knelt to Ulm of Vara, a petty robber holding a barren plain.

Blue Star butted him with her silky nose. The animals of Rhada were unique. Long ago, Emeric claimed (perhaps with provincial pride), the men of the Golden Age had brought the stock of legendary Earth to Rhada, breeding it there for generations to produce the finest chargers in all the galaxy. The Rhadan stallions were far too fierce to be tamed for war, but Rhadan mares bore the warleaders of a hundred planets on their narrow backs.

Blue Star's nostrils dilated at the scent of the open game-bags. She pushed against Glamiss again and said, "Eat, Glamiss. We eat *now*." Her voice was sibilant, the words distinct to a warman accustomed to the language of the mares.

"Go eat, then," he said. "But eat what has already been killed."

Blue Star tossed her narrow head and bared her saber teeth. "Hunt. We hunt."

Glamiss looked at the sky and the distant, disturbed eagles. He did not wish to risk Blue Star in this country of savage birds. "No," he said.

"Hunt," the mare said again.

Glamiss rapped her smartly across the muzzle. "No."

There was a wild light of something resembling amusement in the animal's slotted eyes, as though being struck by a creature she could rend to bloody tatters pleased her, satisfied her need for submission. "Master," she said.

"And tell the Vulk I'm waiting for him."

The mare snorted and bared her teeth again. It was, Glamiss thought, as though she knew that his severe manner toward the Vulk was a pose.

He felt a frailty in himself: too much compassion could be a bad thing for a warleader, and the Vulk—well, they were pitiful things, truly. Small, weak, spindly. Their featureless faces were sad caricatures of men's, and their passive submissiveness could goad men to considerable cruelty. When Vulk were serving in the field as Talkers, many warleaders denied them even the comfort of a mare to ride upon, making them stumble across all sorts of terrain on their sticklike legs behind the warband. Glamiss contended that this was impractical, that there was no advantage in thus slowing the progress of a troop. But Emeric said that it was because sometimes his kindness leaked out between the seams of his armor. "The spirit of the Star is in you, no matter how tough you pretend to be." It was in the high-born Emeric Aulus Kevin Kiersson-Rhad as well, Glamiss had retorted, for though the Order of Navigators was more severe with the Vulk than the mere laity, Nav Emeric treated the alien creatures with courtesy and kindness. Not at all the usual attitude of a priest of the Order toward beings who refused to accept man's religious view of the galaxy.

Glamiss considered his priestly companion, watching him loosening the caparison on Sea Wind before freeing her to join the other mares feeding on the game. The noble Emeric was a member of an Order that formed the only tenuous ties among the worlds of the Great Sky. Navigators were autonomous, ubiquitous. According to the Way—the dogma of their Order —they piloted the starships, served as spiritual counselors to the thousands of petty lordlings on every planet, and acted as military chaplains in the constant warfare. They were needed, Glamiss thought bitterly. On town or village, castle or lodge, the starships might descend at any time, or a troop such as this one might appear. And the Navigators arriving with the invaders would serve with the invaders, while the Navigators of the defenders would serve with the defenders. Navigators never killed Navigators, but they killed others readily enough. And when the fighting was finished, the chaplain of the defeated might pray in the bridge of the invaders' starship, thank God in the Star for his questionable mercy, and return to his wounded, defeated people. The starship would rise into the sky, carrying booty or prisoners. Life would go on as before.

In drunken moments Glamiss would sometimes tax Emeric with this strange evenhandedness in wickedness, and then the Rhadan would patiently explain that the clergy was servant of all God's subjects. If Rhadan fought Vykan and both fought Astrari—did that make them the less God's creatures? The individual Navigator did his duty to his assigned people—the *Order* took no side but God's.

Glamiss asked, "If Vara-Vyka fought the Northern Rhad, would you serve against your own people?"

Emeric's face showed the conflict of blood and faith as he replied, "I would hope the Order would not ask it of me. But if it did, I would then hope that my faith would be strong enough to let me serve God."

It seemed to Glamiss at such times that unless men were once again united, as they had been in the Golden Age, this struggling society of conflict and conflicting loyalties must surely sink into final barbarism.

"You sent for me, Glamiss Warleader."

The speaker was Vulk Asa, a spindly creature no more than a meter and a half high, dressed in fool's motley. The featureless face, eyeless, smoothly modeled from broad, flat cheekbones to a delicate and sensitive mouth, was remarkably mobile and expressive. Glamiss did not believe that men could not read the emotions of the Vulk in their faces. It was rather that men seldom understood what those emotions were, for beyond love and fear, the emotions of the aliens were not those felt by men.

At this moment Glamiss could see that Asa was both weary and apprehensive.

Glamiss said sternly, "Have the troopers been deviling you, Vulk?"

Asa's head, seemingly too large to be supported by his slender neck, wobbled in denial. "No, Warleader."

Emeric had opened his water-bottle. He passed it to the Vulk and said, "Drink, Asa. You look dry."

The Vulk took the flask gratefully and wet his lips.

Glamiss regarded his friend and the Vulk and smiled covertly. The Order of Navigators taught that the Vulk were as they were, eyeless and feeble, because they denied God in the Star. In punishment for that great sin, the demon Cyb had shattered their homeworld in a great astronomical catastrophe, and since that time they had wandered, dispersed and homeless, among the planets of men. The Book of Warls claimed that Vulk lived for twenty thousand years or more, a special refinement of punishment bestowed upon them by Sin —scarcely a thing an educated man would credit, though Glamiss could not remember ever having seen a Vulk dead of old age. They were occasionally killed in pogroms, but natural death was rare.

To the young captain, the disparity between the wicked, aggressive creatures described by The Warls and the Protocols, and the meek aliens he knew Vulk to be cast a certain doubt on the truthfulness of writers. The Vulk existed, after all, on man's charity. In return they amused men—as fools, and served them in the field—as Talkers. Mentally linked to one another over anything less than planetary distances, the Vulk had a certain military value as communicators. But blasphemous, evil, and bloodthirsty as the Protocols claimed? Not likely, Glamiss thought.

"Sit, Asa," he said, less formally now. "Rest."

"I thank you, Glamiss Warleader."

"Look out there," Glamiss said. "What do you see?" The Vulk did not *see* as men did, but their sensitive minds detected the shape of living things, often even the hidden structure of the inanimate.

"There is a settlement, and beyond there is a bridge and a mill. There are fat herds in the meadows. Few men." The Vulk hesitated and then went on. "There is an adept in the valley, Glamiss Warleader."

"A Vulk?"

"No, Warleader. A human being. But—with a special mind. A rare thing now."

"Now?"

The Vulk seemed deliberately vague, as all his kind were when they spoke of the distant past. "There were once many humans with a talent for the mind-touch, Glamiss Warleader. Many died in the killings of the Dark Time."

"The eagles," Glamiss, ever practical, prompted. "Are they under mental control?"

"Partially. Sometimes."

Glamiss made an impatient gesture. "What sort of answer is that, Vulk? I want to know if we must fight the birds as well as the men in the valley."

"I cannot tell you, Warleader. The adept is weak. I think perhaps it is a child. But there is other danger. Beyond the valley—near it—above—an old man—" The words became slurred and jumbled as they often did when the Vulk's strange mind left its body. The creature's muscles twitched and a thin trickle of moisture ran from the slackening mouth.

Emeric seized the thin shoulders and shook Asa sharply. "A warlock? Are the rumors true, Asa?"

"Leave him," Glamiss said shortly. "He will be useless for a bit. Let him rest. And no more about a damned warlock. This is a punitive expedition for Ulm—not a hunt for sinners, Emeric. The Inquisition will have to wait."

A sudden scream, high-pitched and furious, froze the priest and warman where they stood. Higher on the ridge they could see the plunging shape of a Glamiss's war mare, Blue Star, rearing and striking with her clawed feet at a huge, leathery-winged bird that had appeared from high above. As they watched, the eagle rose and stooped again, the broad wings almost covering the raging mare.

Glamiss and Emeric scrambled up the slope, the priest calling for Sea Wind. Already the rogue eagle had opened several red gashes on Blue Star's heaving flank. As they watched, the mare ripped at the wing-membranes of her attacker, screaming with fury.

Sea Wind galloped toward the Navigator and he swung into the saddle with the swift ease of a Rhadan. He let his mount carry him ahead of Glamiss and under the menacing wings of the dragonlike bird. His long iron sword was in his hand and he struck at a descending talon with all his strength. The eagle uttered a shrill cry and beat at him with razor-tipped wings. His blow had severed the eagle's foot, and the bloody stump crashed wetly against his iron mail, almost unhorsing him.

Glamiss reached the battle now, his flail swinging. A slash from the eagle's remaining foot sent him tumbling among the rocks. Emeric could hear the clatter of troopers running to their assistance, but the great bird's beak was suddenly darting at his unprotected face and he raised a mailed arm to protect himself and murmured an Ave Stella, for he felt very close to death.

He heard the wicked whirring of iron chains and the solid *chunk* of the morningstars, the spiked balls of the flail, striking the bird's armored head. When he could look again, the eagle was down, its neck broken by Glamiss's flail. A furious and bloody-flanked Blue Star was ripping at the fallen, already dying monster with her clawed feet.

He reeled in the saddle and held onto Sea Wind's arching neck. The troopers clattered up to them and stood looking respectfully at the twitching, dying bird.

Glamiss was inspecting his mare's injuries, cursing and blaspheming in a steady stream. It seemed to him that his question about having to fight the great birds had been answered. If the adept in the valley had sent the eagle, the troop's situation was perilous. He gentled the still excited Blue Star, rubbing her silky muzzle and murmuring to her. Had a *child* done this? Anything seemed possible in this strange valley.

Abruptly, he made up his mind. He turned away and scrambled down the ridge to where Asa still sat, half-recovered now from the effort of his mental probe of the valley.

"Asa," he said, "there is more in this place than fifty warmen can handle. Tell Rahel that we must have a starship with the full warband from Vara."

"Rahel, yes," the Vulk said vaguely, smiling. He would reach across the miles in the Vulk's way, Glamiss knew, to touch the mind of his sister-wife, the Vulk Rahel, who remained always in the keep on the plain. Asa and Rahel were the two termini of the Talk, the only communication at a distance this world knew.

Emeric was at his shoulder, protesting. "Ulm will never let you lead the full warband. He would not dare."

"Then let him come himself. I need more men."

Emeric studied his friend's intent face. It was certainly not fear that had done this to Glamiss. The Vykan was without fear. But there was an instinct in him that Emeric had often seen. Glamiss was a military genius. Perhaps even a political one. There was something in the valley of Trama Glamiss wanted, something he must have. Emeric suspected that it might be knowledge—forbidden knowledge. He shivered inwardly, thinking not of the bumbling, crude Ulm—but of the Inquisition. He said, "There is no starship at Vara. There will be none until the *Gloria in Coelis* arrives from Aurora."

"Then let Ulm send the soldiers overland. I must have more men."

"Enough to take and hold this valley for yourself, warleader?" Emeric asked evenly. "You know that if there is sin in Trama, it is for the Order Militant to say what must be done about it."

Glamiss's eyes were as cold as the glacier on the mountain. His words were both treasonous and blasphemous, but Emeric had no doubt whatever that he meant them. "Whatever there is here I will have, Emeric—if I must wade through blood to get it."

The Navigator's voice was steady. "Even if the blood is mine, Glamiss?"

The Vykan's expression tightened and he said, "Even then, old friend," and turned to climb the ridge once again.

Chapter Five

The cosmography of the Second Stellar Empire is based, of course, on that of the First Empire. Confusion has arisen, however, due to the much greater size of the domain of the Rigellian Galactons, which needed to be divided into Marches, Provinces, Sectors, and finally the stellar systems with which we are familiar. In ancient times, for example, the Province of Vega contained at least a dozen star systems known as "Vega." Local names were used by the natives, but the Imperial Cosmographic Institute listed these systems as Vega A, B, C, and so on. (These classifications should not be confused with the "Alpha," "Beta," etc., used to differentiate between stars of multiple systems.) Confusion has been compounded by the Second Empire practice of renaming certain star systems, corrupting the old names of others, and retaining the Golden Age names of still others. Thus modern Vega and Vyka lie within the ancient Province of Vega but are separate and distinct star systems seven parsecs apart. This, in spite of the fact that "Vyka" is nothing more nor less than an Interregnal corruption of the name "Vega." Cosmographers tell us that present-day Vega and modern Vyka were, in ancient times, Vega B and Vega C, respectively.

—Star Commander Kendo alt Styglyz, *First Principles of Cosmogation,* Late Second Stellar Empire period

It is told in the dark forests that the evil princes of Cyb and Sin who plotted against the god-men of the Golden Age had the power to light the suns and strike terror into the hearts of all men. This they did for joy of wickedness, and their wickedness grew apace and they grew over-proud and they enlarged their wickedness until the very stars were consumed and the Dark Time was upon all the worlds of the Great Sky.

—From *The Book of Warls,* Interregnal period

Shana Lar faced her father with tear-stained cheeks. The talon mark on her upper arm had stopped leaking blood and subsided to an ugly brownish smear. She tugged nervously at her straight-combed hair and covered her small, naked breasts courteously as she waited on her knees for the head of the household to come to a decision about the thing the eagles had seen.

Shevil, gray and weathered, old at forty seasons, tugged half-heartedly at the ritual seams in his weyr skin vest, and prayed to the Star for guidance. Behind him, arranged in a council semicircle, squatted the six elders of the valley. Shevil was aware that the youngest, Tamil Hind, was being distracted from his deliberations by the sight of Shana's sweaty skin and scratched, but shapely thighs. With one portion of his mind Shevil concentrated on the momentous decision the folk expected of the elders, and with another—that part that devoted itself to the business of being the father of four daughters and no sons—pondered the possibility of marrying Shana to Tamil, who owned a substantial number of the weyr in the high pastures.

Actually, Shevil was angry with Shana: angry but relieved

that she had come to no real harm by disobeying him and join-
ing the eagles' convocation on the stone cliff. He was also
dubious about Tamil's honorable intentions regarding her, for
she was an adept and no man of the valley of Trama ever willingly married a mutation. None, Shevil thought dourly, save
Shevil Lar, and he remembered Shana's mother; Shevaughn
of the slotted, silver eyes and six fingers, whom he had taken
to wife (in spite of all his father could do to discourage him)
and loved deeply for the five warm years she lived. Did Tamil
understand that women whose ancestors had stood in the light
of the Falling Sun seldom lived to be old?

But Shana was waiting and so were the others, and outside
the hovel stood fully half of the half-hundred folk of the
valley. They expected wisdom and a plan to keep them safe
from the warmen the eagles had seen. Shevil frowned and
drew a deep breath. What they actually wanted was for him to
cut the throat of a prime weyr and lead them all up the
moraine to seek the sorcerer who lived inside the deadly mountain, that was *really* what they wanted. The folk had become
querulous and dependent on the Warlock, who had appeared
three seasons back from within the belly of the mountain.
They had lost their self-dependence, expecting always to be
protected by the blind spirit-man's magic.

But that was exactly the point and the danger, Shevil argued
with himself. The eagles had seen a Navigator with Vara's
warmen, and that meant that the ways of the folk were
known, somehow, to the grim priests of the Inquisition. To
turn to the Warlock in this extremity would be to damn the
settlement and all who lived in it forever. The Navigator
would know and the warmen would erect a burning stake in
the meadow. Shevil imagined his daughters screaming in the
fire and shivered. In truth it was Shana he saw in his mind's
eye, for she had always been his favorite child. Gytha, Marya,
and Arietee were dull girls, very much creatures of the valley.
But Shana was like dark quicksilver, and his love.

Behind him, Quarlo the miller, cleared his throat and said
tentatively, "Time is passing, Shevil. We listened to you three
seasons ago and held back Lord Ulm's weyr-tribute. Now that
his warmen have come, you must tell us what you intend for us
to do."

The resentment, though hidden, was discernible in his voice.

It was true, Shevil thought, that he had counseled the folk to keep their weyr. He had heard from a traveler that Ulm was at war across the Narrow Sea and that year the winter had been bitter, so that the folk of Trama might have died of hunger had the tribute been sent. And then the second year and the third? Shevil asked himself. Well, once the old patterns had been broken, once Ulm's rights had been denied, it seemed easier to withhold the tribute for another year, and then another. And there had been the appearance of the Warlock—yes, one had to consider that, too. To excuse himself and his counsel of rebellion, Shevil had declared that the appearance of the mad old spirit from the mountain had been an omen of approval from the Star—

Lies, all lies, Shevil thought bitterly. Not the Star, but Sin and Cyb had sent the Warlock, and he, Shevil Lar, had known it in his heart from the beginning. Now the folk waited for him to save them from the results of his sinful folly.

"You are certain the eagles saw a priest, Shana?"

The girl answered with averted eyes as was proper when addressing the elders, even though the hetman was her father. "Yes, Shevil. A priest and, I think, one of the tiny men. I can't be sure of that. The eagles do not know them. But I think I felt one near."

A Vulk, Shevil thought. Worse and worse. Long ago, in his young manhood, when he had dreamed of being a mercenary soldier, he had traveled to one of the outposts of the Lord Ulm's warband. His journey had been a failure because the soldiers had laughed at him and beaten him with their sheathed swords, making sport of the peasant who wished to carry iron weapons. But he had seen a Vulk: eyeless, noseless, hideous to view—a creature with terrible mental powers, far more potent and dark than those of any mutation. The soldiers had told him that the Vulk could touch minds across thousands of kilometers of ocean and mountain, that he could turn humans to stone with an incantation, that he ate the hearts of children and drank women's blood. All that and much more, as the Protocols explained, were gifts to the Vulkish people from their masters the Adversaries, Sin and Cyb.

"Are you certain about this thing, Shana?" he asked. "A Navigator would not travel with a Vulk."

"I have heard of them being together," Tamil Hind interjected. "The priests have spells that can enslave the creatures. Sometimes they break free and then the Navigator is damned, but I have heard of this thing Shana's eagles saw."

"The eagles did not see a Vulk," Shana said rudely. She did not like Tamil devouring her with his eyes, seeking her favor by telling tales like this one. "I sensed something strange. It could have been one of them, that is all." She turned her eyes, so silvery gray they reminded Shevil of Shevaughn's, on her father. "Tell us what we must do, Shevil. The Navigator will burn us."

The others broke out in angry murmurs of agreement. They muttered of the Warlock, as Shevil knew they would.

Still, what else was there? Half a hundred herdsmen and women could not defend themselves against the Lord Ulm's warmen. Damnation had fallen upon them with the coming of the Warlock. But death as rebels was more real, and it was coming upon them from the southern ridge of the valley, probably with the rise of the sun. "Very well," the hetman said, "we will go to the mountain"—he paused and swallowed the bitter taste of fear—"and there we will seek the protection of Sin and Cyb." He said over his shoulder to Tamil, "Snare a fat weyr for sacrifice," then he turned to the other elders. Their dull, stupid faces made him ache with anger. Was the world always like this, he wondered? Had there ever been a life without fear? Had there ever been, in fact, a Golden Age —and if so, would there ever be again?

Heavily, he said, "Perhaps the flesh of the weyr will please the Warlock, but I must tell you that I do not believe he cares for such things. If he is a true son of Sin and Cyb, his price for saving us may be much greater."

He raised his daughter to her feet and spoke to the folk who crowded about his open doorway. "Go and make ready. A member of each family must climb the moraine with the elders." He stroked Shana's dark hair and said, "Dress in your best, daughter, and cover yourself. The Warlock must not think us savages." And he thought of a line from The Warls: *From the wrath of the warmen, who will deliver us?* Who, indeed, he wondered bitterly.

* * *

On the ridge, where the soldiers bivouacked, the cooking fires burned low. Glamiss prowled the outposts studying the sky for further attacks from the eagles of Trama. But the birds seemed to have vanished from the sky and now, as evening drew near, a thin skin of high clouds began to cover the sun and the wind turned bitterly cold as it blew across the ice-fields and snowy peaks of the northern mountains.

At the picket line he stopped to inspect Blue Star's injuries once again. The mare was still nervous and angry and she showed her teeth at his approach, scratching at the hard ground with her deadly claws.

"Fight," she said. "Fight the flying things, Glamiss."

"Soon," the Vykan said.

Blue Star shook her head savagely and snorted. Idly, Glamiss stroked the soft, dark, furred skin of her muzzle. The mares would suffer if there was a freeze in the night. They were a hardy breed, accustomed to the grassy plains of Rhada where they were born, but they were lowland animals, bred for thousand of years on sea-level tundras. On Rhada, only the polar islands ever froze; the continents had a cold but even climate.

For a time Glamiss pondered the peculiar similarities and strange differences of the animal forms he knew. The horses of Rhada, like Blue Star, Sea Wind, and the others of this troop, were light-boned, swift beasts. Their eyes were pale blue—the color of turquoise—with slit pupils. Like many other of the life-forms with which the warman was familiar, they were rudimentarily telepathic (according to Emeric, bred to it so that they would obey their warrior without bit or bridle in battle) and possessed of a simple language. Yet on Vegan worlds, horses were much larger, less intelligent, and heavily armored with chitinous plates like those of insects, or armored lizards. How had this come about, Glamiss wondered. The legends said that the men of the Golden Age, expanding into the galaxy from mythic Earth, had taken with them the life-essence of many Earth animals, and from this source had bred the beasts to suit their strange needs on alien planets. Perhaps it was so, though *how* the thing was done was beyond imagining. For a thoughtful moment he tried to imagine the men of the Empire boarding the great starships laden with their sinful packets of life. Had there been an Order of Navigators then? Priests believed it, or said they did. But Glamiss did not. No, in those days there could have been no priesthood and the piloting of starships must have been done by ordinary men. The young warman tried to imagine what Earth must have been like (if it existed at all, that is)—a world of gold and silver avenues and jeweled buildings circling a diamond sun situated in the exact center of the galaxy, 333,333 kilometers to the Rim of the Great Sky in all directions. The orderliness of such a society seemed utopian to Glamiss and quite unreal. But the idea of so many millions of people living and working together in amity and safety was strangely moving. Even if it never was, actually, that way—it should have been, he thought.

Nav Emeric, his robe hitched up to show his mail-clad legs, appeared from the direction of the bivouac. He had stripped off his weapons and unlaced the throat of his iron-chain shirt, and he carried a cup of hot bouillon and a strip of broiled meat.

"Have you eaten? Here." He offered the rations to Glamiss, who took them silently.

"I have been thinking of what you said, Glamiss," the priest said in a low voice. "What, exactly, do you think we will find down there?" He indicated the valley, in shadow now.

"I don't know," Glamiss replied. "But there is something there. Things we have never seen before, perhaps. I can't explain it. It is as though we've stumbled on something I need to know—something I must have before—" He broke off suddenly and the Navigator studied his somber face intently.

"There is a strangeness in you, Glamiss Warleader," Emeric said. "I felt it from the first day we met. You are different from other men of our time."

Glamiss raised his eyebrows. "Why do you say 'from other men of our time'?"

"A feeling, no more. Vulk Asa senses it, too. We've spoken of it together."

"You have discussed me with the Vulk?"

The Navigator smiled wryly. "Terrible, is it not? But there it is. It might be blasphemous to say so, but it is almost as though you have been chosen for something. Have you never wondered at how men follow you so willingly? Don't you think it strange that a man of your humble birth should come so far as you have?"

"The thought has occurred to me," Glamiss said in a dry tone.

"Forgive me, my friend. But you asked me. Why, you come from a tribe that isn't even allowed to bear arms, isn't that so?"

"It is," Glamiss said. "My people are herdsmen. Like those." He turned his eyes on the darkening valley.

"Yet now you are the most honored warleader in Ulm's warband. Has it never come to you that perhaps there is the hand of God in the Star in this?"

Glamiss grinned ruefully. "I thought you would give the credit to the Adversaries."

"I'm not joking, Glamiss," the Navigator said soberly. "You must be a chosen one. Though chosen for what, I cannot say."

Glamiss narrowed his eyes against the fading light and thought of his recurring dream. He said quietly, "In the night, sometimes, I see myself standing on an island between two rivers, Nav Emeric. In my hands are a flail and dagger. On my back a feathered cloak. And on my head a circlet of gold—"

Emeric turned pale, but did not speak.

Glamiss, unaware, went on in that strange, still voice. "There are starships in my dream, a sky filled with them. And behind me a warband—but a greater warband than I have ever seen—an army with strange banners." He smiled slowly and turned to look at his friend. "What do you make of that, friend priest?"

The Navigator was silent for what seemed a long time. He knew, without knowing why he knew it, that he must speak with great care and precision, for he was certain that the spirit of the Star was nearby.

"Glamiss," he said evenly, "what do you know of Nyor?"

"The Queen City of the Stars? What everyone knows. That it does not exist. That it probably never existed. It is like Earth, a legend—no more. Or perhaps, less romantically, it was simply the capital of the lost Empire."

"Nyor exists, Glamiss Warleader. Nyor has always existed," the Navigator said. "I have spoken with starship

Navigators who have *been* there. It is far off across the Great Sky, and it lies in ruins now. But it once stood on an island between two rivers, Glamiss. The island is called Manhat, and the Galactons ruled from that place. They ruled for five thousand years, Glamiss, and their symbols were the flail, the dagger, and the feathered cape.''

Glamiss stared at the priest with cold eyes; his face seemed suddenly to have been cut from stone. "Don't joke with me, priest. We are friends, but don't joke with me about this thing. It is not a matter to use lightly.''

"As the Star is my witness, I speak the truth," the Rhadan said.

"How does it happen I have never heard of it?''

"It is Navigators' knowledge—not for the unconsecrated man.''

"And yet you tell it to me?''

The Navigator nodded slowly. "In violation of my vows, Glamiss. May the Star forgive me, but there are times when a priest is also a man. I told you I believe you are a chosen one. Perhaps it has been given to me to recognize you for what you will become. I know no reason I should be given such grace— I'm not a very good priest. I'm too proud by half, and far too worldly. I'll never be a saint. But I know what I know. I can feel it, here, inside my guts. One day, you *will* wear the feathered cape, Glamiss. It will probably take your lifetime—and mine. But the *time* is right for a great conqueror. There's been too long a night, my friend. And I believe you are the man. So I violate my vows. I should feel shame, perhaps, but I feel none.'' He turned away and stood on the edge of the ridge, looking not down into the valley of Trama, but up at the sky where the light was slowly going, and where the sparse stars of the Vykan night would soon shine feebly through the thin clouds. "That is why I will serve you, Glamiss Warleader—down there in the valley tomorrow, or across the Great Sky when that time comes.''

The Vykan grasped the Navigator's shoulders and managed a half-smile. "We're both mad, you know. It must be this place.''

Emeric shook his head somberly. "I know one other thing. There will come a time when I must again choose between you and my Order. The choice I make then may not be the choice I make tonight. But that will be many years from now—in Nyor.''

Vulk Asa huddled by one of the fires and turned his blind face toward the two figures conversing in the fading light. He heard one of the warmen laugh and speak to his battle-partner.

"Look at them up there, will you? Glamiss and the priest, settling the hash of the whole bloody world.''

The Vulk smiled inwardly. He had seen it all happen before in the course of his race's group-life. Passive, directed by forces humans would not begin to understand for a million years, the Vulk had seen the wheel of history turn many times. *We watch,* Vulk Asa thought, *and we wish you well. But we do not interfere.*

And across the miles he felt the caressing touch of his sister-wife's thought: *Guide them gently and they will go far.*

Chapter Six

Conditions will be so terrible that no man will be able to lead a decent life. Then will all the sorrows of the Apocalypse pour down upon mankind: Flood, Earthquake, Pestilence and Famine; neither shall the crops grow nor the fruits ripen; the wells will dry up and the waters will bear upon them blood and bitterness, so that the birds of the air, the beasts in the field and the fishes in the sea will all perish.

—From the *Nürnburg Chronicle* (AD 1493 Old Style) Middle Dawn Age period

The cyclic repetitions of human history fill me with a sense of *déjà vu*. I am the mightiest of men—and the most frightened.

—Attributed to Rigell XXVIII, last Galacton of the First Stellar Empire

In his drugged sleep of dreams, the old man who had been Ophir ben Rigell ibn Sol alt Messier, Nephew and Heir to the Great Throne, Lord of the Sky Isles and the Marches, Prince of Rhada and High Duke of Cygnus, Amir of Tau Ceti and

King-Elector of the Empire, could both see and remember.

His robe, on orders from the hospital computer, administered his maintenance dose of trilaudid each time he slept. The regimen was an improvisation, for the hospital computer having waited in vain for centuries, for someone to tell it how to cure the old man's addiction and drug-induced blindness could prescribe nothing better. Once the patient was taken from the cold Sleep, the withdrawal of the drug would kill him—and he was too old to be put back in the vaults. He could not again be wakened.

The effect of trilaudid was, in its early stages, a feeling of well-being and euphoria. The user became aware of intense pleasure in every physical and mental activity, and the unpleasant aspects of life were transmuted into sources of joy. The Lord Ophir had, long before coming to the vaults of the cold Sleep, passed through that stage. He had entered the final stages of addiction in which the trilaudid addict began to shut down his sensory extensions into the real world, the more fully to appreciate the delights to be enjoyed inwardly. The first faculty to go was generally sight, and so it had been in the case of Lord Ophir. He had been almost totally blind before the Lady Dihanna (at the Lord Rigell's insistence) had prevailed upon Ophir to take the Sleep.

Cannily, he had known even as he boarded the *Delos* that night, millennia ago, that her real purpose had been to store him until some cure for his addiction (rather than merely his blindness, which was but a symptom) could be found.

In his alert dream, at his own choice, he relived those days. He remembered that trilaudid addiction had been widespread among the lords and nobles of the Empire. That "unimportant" civil conflict on the Rim had been, in fact, unimportant only to an aristocracy and a large upper-middle class removed from reality by trilaudid and its derivatives. The Inner Worlds had been gutted of purpose or discipline by their own popular, drug-oriented, and permissive culture. A few nobles—Dihanna had been one of them—had striven for a rebirth of discipline. Ophir considered this with dreamy pleasure: they had obviously failed. The Empire was no more.

With trilaudid rerouting the electrical impulses of his brain, Ophir could survey the softly featureless landscape of his memories with joy. Even the knowledge that in his waking state he would be irritable to the point of paranoia, that his memory would be paralyzed, that his blindness would force him to rely on the prosthetic eye he wore—all this gave him drug-pleasure. For it assured him that he would turn to sleep again—the sleep of trilaudid.

Dihanna, he thought dreamily, and his pleasure-sharpened mind recreated her. He touched her glossy ebony skin, felt the tight, wiry texture of her flame-colored hair. She seemed to be saying: "You see, I *did* join you after all, Ophir." And: "I was wrong, wrong to oppose pleasure and happiness and love—" Some ancient flicker of reality sparked in his brain, and for just an instant he knew that he was with a false Dihanna, that she would never have spoken so about drug-happiness. But almost instantly, the trilaudid in his bloodstream blunted the single synapse, and Dihanna became once again the soft, acquiescent creature his addiction had made her.

His uncle, the Galacton, said: "You are the heir, Ophir. You cannot—" The mere suggestion of the word "cannot" triggered the drug reaction again, and the Galacton smiled down at his favorite nephew from the Great Star Throne and said, "Yes, of course, yes—whatever gives you pleasure, my young lion—"

The images darkened, faded. The computer had detected visitors at the tunnel mouth and, knowing they sought the Warlock, was waking him. Lord Ophir fought to keep to his drug-dream, but the computer was immune to the ethic of trilaudid: "Whatever gives you pleasure, do." It turned his robe cold and he awoke. Bitterness overwhelmed him. Once again he could not remember his own name. His brain seemed to have ceased to function. He felt half-alive as the infusion of the drug slowed, a million tiny needles withdrawing from his withered flesh.

He opened his electronic eye. On the telescreen above his sleep-tank the computer had projected the scene in the moraine.

The villagers of Trama were there in force. Torches burned, though the last light had not yet faded from the sky. They were chanting dark verses from that mess of superstition they called The Warls.

The computer said, "Go. It is good for you to see other humans."

The Warlock snarled, "Humans? Savages. Beasts."

The computer made no distinctions. It was concerned only with the well-being of its patient, and it had been told, aeons ago, that without contact with others of his kind, man, the social animal, withers and dies.

"It is bad therapy for a patient to refuse visitors when he is able to see them," the recorded voice said.

"Why do they bother me?" the Warlock asked, rising unwillingly from the tank.

The question was recognized as rhetorical and not answered.

"Why *me*?" This time an answer was wanted. But the hospital computer's billion software packages did not include anything pertinent to skin-wearing savages in the hospital valley. Instead, like any doctor, it said, "It will do you good to see them."

The Warlock's eyes, dark with trilaudid blindness, jerked and trembled. *"Who am I?"* he burst out hopelessly.

This information the computer did have, but it was considered poor therapy to present trilaudid addicts with contradictions. The computer, again like any doctor, lied for the patient's good. "I am not programmed to answer that. When the doctor comes, he will decide what must be done."

"The doctor is never coming!" the old man screamed. *"No one is coming—ever!"*

"You have visitors," the computer said primly. And then, with maddening electronic smugness, repeated, "It is bad therapy for a patient to refuse visitors when he is able to—"

The Warlock fled from the room.

In the deepening dusk, Shevil Lar led the villagers in the litany, the chant from the Warls.

> "From the rage of the star-raiders,
> Save us!"

The torch-lit faces, raised in supplication to the blank and
empty tunnel mouth, swayed in the flame-brightness. The
response came like a rumble on the wind from the mountains.

> *"Salve!"*
> "From the fire in the sky,
> Protect us!"
> *"Salve dominus!"*

The language was the ancient tongue, a slurred and cor-
rupted thing filled with the clicks and elisions of the Old
Anglic of the Empire and mingled with words and phrases
borrowed from languages still more ancient, their origins lost
in the mists of the Dawn Age.

> "O Warlock, filled with wisdom,
> Protect us!"
> *"Salve, rey de la noche!"*

Shevil raised his torch and made the Dark Sign, the Star
with Four Points, the Cross of Night, that summoned warlocks and propitiated both Sin and Cyb. The tunnel mouth remained empty and Shevil was filled with a hopeless despair.
The Warlock was capricious, and he, Shevil, had warned the
folk that he might not come.

The bearded faces of the men in the first circle were unreadable in the torch light. But the women who stood behind them
were afraid and their faces showed it. It was the women who
had been most willing to accept the gifts of Sin and Cyb from
the creature who lived under the glacier: the mill, the new ways
to heal the sick, even the training of Shana's gift to curb the
marauding eagles. The women were afraid of the priest-Navigator who Shana said rode with the warmen of the Lord Ulm,
but they were even more frightened at the thought that the
Warlock might now choose simply to forget the folk of Trama
valley.

Shevil said, "Bring the weyr."

The men carried the struggling animal spread-eagled. Its
soft dark eyes were fearful. It knew it was meeting its death,
Shevil realized. But what good would it do? The fly-blown

carcass of the last sacrifice to the Warlock of the mountain still lay where they had left it on their last meeting here. The rotting smell of it tainted the cold evening wind.

"Shana."

Shevil's daughter carried the knife. It was an ancient weapon, intricately carved and damascened with scenes of strange battle on its bright blade. The pommel had been worked in soft yellow metal into the flaming Star and Spaceship of the Old People. It had been brought by the folk to the valley in time past, during one of the migrations from the plains. Shevil's great-great-grandfather was said to have found it in the night-glowing ruins of some ancient battlefield, a place where the Suns fell. It was said among the people that the old man, the first Shevil Lar, had sickened and died after his blasphemous invasion of that blasted place. His hair had turned gray and fallen away in patches, and he had weakened and had known no peace, so great was the taboo. And finally, he had died and none could save him. There was no one even to try, for he had been shaman in those days, the healer of the sick folk, and if he could not save himself, then no man could.

But the folk had kept the knife-that-burns and the next generation of Lars had been a short one, for the knife carried with it a strong taboo and curse from Sin and Cyb. The Adversaries always exacted a blood-price.

Even now, it was unwise to hold the knife too long, lest the touch of the god-metal raise blisters on the skin. Only Shana, who was strange in other ways as well, could carry the knife.

With his hands on his daughter's shoulders, Shevil followed the men and the weyr up the path they had worn in the rubble of the moraine to the tunnel-mouth. In the torchlight, Shevil could make out the symbols cut into the god-metal rim of the open doorway. They were the glyphs of the Empire, spiky and evilly shaped. They formed a legend Shevil could neither read nor understand: *Cryonic Storage D*. And below the large symbol, a rank of smaller ones, like soldiers following a war-leader, Shevil thought. *Emergency Access, Radiation Shelter*. Ugly shapes, like nothing seen in nature, and consequently the work, beyond a doubt, of Sin and Cyb.

Shevil guided Shana carefully, feeling the tension in her young flesh under his hands. It was Shana who knew the

Warlock best, for she had spent many hours with him at the machines, actually within the mountain. But even she was afraid, and Shevil wondered, did she fear the sin the folk had committed or was her fear like that of the other women, a dread of facing the warmen without the Warlock's magic?

Shana the Dark, the hetman thought. *Shana the witch. My daughter. We are an accursed family among an accursed folk. When that first Shevil went to the place where a Sun fell, he divided our blood from salvation. Long ago,* he thought, *the folk should have driven us out to freeze on the glacier—*

"Father—"

"Don't speak, Shana. It is not fitting."

The girl followed the men with the struggling, bleating weyr up the path through the smooth rocks and pebbles of the moraine. Shevil Lar noted that young Tamil was one of the men. He frowned, knowing the fellow must have bribed one of the elders more senior than he to let him take the burden to the top of the path. One more thing improperly done, Shevil Lar thought grimly. The younger generation was without respect for anything. Tamil shall not have Shana for wife, Shevil decided. And then he suppressed an impulse to smile bitterly, for this was surely no time to think of such things. If the Warlock did not appear, by tomorrow's sunset the folk might be charred flesh at the burning stakes. The Order of Navigators was without mercy on sinners who dealt with the powers of Sin and Cyb.

"But, father," Shana whispered agitatedly, "Shevil—"

"Hush, girl."

His daughter shook her head angrily. "I must tell you, Shevil. One of the eagles has attacked the warmen on the ridge. A rogue bird, father. But the attack will lead the tiny man directly to me. He will know I have the mind-touch."

Shevil's heart felt heavy in his chest. It seemed, after all, that God in the Star had *not* forgotten the folk of Trama. He watched from the Great Sky, just as the Navigators said, and made his terrible judgments. He knew that Sin and Cyb had taken root in the valley. And no matter how much the Adversaries might wish to remain hidden in these mountains, they had not been able to prevent the rogue bird's attack which would warn the priest-Navigator on the ridge that all was not what it seemed to be in the valley of Trama. The stakes and the fire seemed very close to Shevil Lar and the folk at this moment, and he shuddered, knowing that they were now totally committed to the Warlock and at the mercy of his Cybish capriciousness. *"Salve rey de la noche,"* he murmured, "appear to us or we are truly lost."

At the low step of god-metal before the dark tunnel mouth the men stopped and lifted the weyr, head down and still struggling, for the folk to see. The chanting began again, this time with more urgency.

> "The starships come and the warbands gather,
> Save us, Dark Fathers!
> What have we done to suffer fire and sword?
> Save us, wise Warlocks!
> From across the Sky the star kings send us death!
> *Strike them, Night Fathers!"*

"The knife, daughter," Shevil Lar said.

The cold metal seemed to burn on his palm. He faced the blank tunnel mouth and said simply, "We offer you what we have, Dark Father."

With a single movement, he cut the weyr's throat and in the flickering torchlight black blood gushed from the wound, splashing like oil on the metal step. Shevil felt the warmth of it on his sandaled feet and suppressed a shudder.

The men threw the still quivering carcass to the ground and waited. The chanting broke into rumbling and then subsided into a kind of silence as the folk continued to wait. In the stillness, Shevil Lar could hear the wind sighing through the feathery trees in the lower valley and the distant ripple of sound from the flowing river. Night sounds, and the soft communal breathing of the folk, silenced by the sight and smell of blood running like a freshet through the rocks down the moraine.

But the Warlock did not appear.

For the space of a hundred heartbeats, the tribe waited. But the tunnel mouth remained dark and empty.

Below, the women began to wail with despair and the men muttered.

A voice called out. *"It was not enough."*

Shevil felt the beginnings of a cold, very personal dread. The traditional sacrifice to the Adversaries was animal blood. But it had not always been so. In the darkest age of the Dark Time, Sin and Cyb had required richer drink and all the folks knew it, as did Shevil Lar.

"It was not enough!" the same voice came again. And this time there were others acquiescing, urging. Shevil shivered and thought: *Little wonder the Suns fell. Men and women are abominations. . . .*

"The Warlock demands more, Shevil!"

Shevil stood frozen, knowing now what the folk demanded of him. Had it always been so in the past, he wondered? Was the price of hetmanship so high? There were legends, some so ancient they were legends in the Golden Age, of leaders made to sacrifice of their own blood to propitiate the wind or the soil or the sky. Shevil's mother had told him the timeless tale of Great Agamemnon, a warleader whose fleet of starships would not rise from the sea, held there by Sin and Cyb, until he gave them to drink of his daughter Iphigenia's blood. Shevil shuddered, remembering how that Star King was struck down by the Star in the person of an adulterous wife. . . . He closed his eyes and wished with all his heart that he could pray to the Star now, that he had not damned himself by his devil-worship, that he could take Shana by the hand and run from this place.

He heard a woman's voice screaming from below. "Tamil! The Warlock wants *her* blood! Take her, Tamil!" The voice was Arietee's, Shevil thought with dismay. He held Shana's shoulders in a viselike grip, remembering his silver-eyed Shevaughn, who had warned him that the folk hated what was strange and would turn on him if he refused to believe it.

"Father—?" Shana said.

Shevil Lar shook his head sharply. "Pay them no mind, daughter. It's madness."

"Tamil! Shana!"

Others below were taking up the cry, calling for deeper

sacrifice from their hetman. *"Give him Shana!"*

Quarlo the miller and Tamil stared at one another uneasily, then at Shevil Lar and his daughter.

Shevil raised the knife-that-burns and said, "Don't even think it. Stay where you are."

"But, Shevil," the miller said reasonably, "if the Warlock does not come, we are dead men. All of us."

Tamil looked at Shana and licked his lips. Shevil could see the strange conflict on his face.

"If you take a step toward her, I swear I'll kill you both," Shevil said.

From below the cries rose up, fearful, lustful, furious at this check. *"Shana! Let it be Shana!"*

Quarlo leaned. Shevil glanced quickly from him back to Tamil. The young man had decided. The decision was on his face, in his eyes. He moved, and Shevil swung Shana behind him and crouched, knife held sword-fashion, low, pointed at Tamil's belly. The others backed away, all but Quarlo, who had his own knife bared.

The miller began to circle, to take Shevil from the flank, but the moraine was narrow here and the light uncertain. Shevil felt the fury building in him. These would take his daughter from him, spill her blood in sacrifice—and for what? He bared his teeth and howled with rage and despair.

Tamil lunged, but his foot slipped in the blood of the weyr and Shevil's point raked across his chest making a shallow cut. Tamil screamed with pain and fright.

Shevil heard the sharp intake of breath from the folk below, and the sudden silence.

Shana shielded her eyes and dropped to her knees, "The Warlock, father! The Warlock!"

Shevil raised his eyes to the tunnel mouth which was now suddenly and miraculously a blaze of light. The Warlock stood there, his terrible eyes staring, his mouth open and red in his grizzled beard. The silver cloak he wore seemed to shimmer and rustle with his anger.

His voice, amplified by the gown that sensed his every need, reverberated and crashed down the mountainside.

"Animals! Savages! What are you doing now! How dare you come to this place with your swine's battles! Filth! Blood-

lovers! God curse you—put up your weapons!"

The burning eye lowered its view to take in the slaughtered weyr and the Warlock's frame seemed to shiver and tremble with fury. "Take that *thing* away from me! Take it away at once!" He turned and would have retreated into the tunnel once again, but Shevil leaped onto the god-metal step and, dragging Shana with him, threw himself at the Warlock's feet.

"They wanted me to sacrifice my daughter, Dark Prince! They said the weyr was not enough!"

The Warlock stopped in midstride and stood for a moment, as though transfixed. His wizened face was a mask of horror and disgust. Then his expression softened slightly as he murmured, "Dihanna? Is it you, Dihanna?" Shevil Lar rose to his feet and pressed himself and Shana against the strangely smooth wall of the tunnel. His heart was fluttering and pounding like a living thing. Quarlo and the bleeding Tamil were following the others in a mad rush down the moraine.

Shana stood very still while the muttering, humming eye examined her. She shivered as she saw how it seemed to grow, like a second, smaller head from the Warlock's shoulder.

"No," the Lord Ophir said more calmly. "You are not Dihanna. You are the bird girl from the village."

"Yes, sire," Shana whispered.

"They wanted to *sacrifice* you? Cut your throat?" An expression of fastidious disbelief suffused the old face. "To *me?"*

Shevil would have spoken, but the Warlock silenced him with a gesture.

"Yes, Dark Prince," Shana said.

"Unbelievable," the Warlock said. "Are you savages, then? Have you sunk to human sacrifice?" He shook his head and murmured to himself in an unknown language.

Shevil, who could not forget that he was hetman of Trama, said, "They are frightened, Lord. The warmen of Ulm have come."

"Good," the Warlock said sharply. "Let them do their duty. Are they less savages than you?" His tone conveyed an impregnable superiority. It was in such a voice, Shevil thought, that a man might address a crawling insect—a lower form of life.

"They will kill us, Lord. There is a priest with them," Shevil said, pleadingly.

"Those who rebel against their rulers deserve nothing better," the Warlock said in that imperial voice.

"They would not punish us that way for rebellion, Dark Lord," Shana said evenly. "But for worshipping *you*."

The Warlock stiffened. He raised his hands to his head and muttered again in the unknown tongue.

"We do not understand you, Lord," Shevil Lar said desperately.

"Of course you don't," the Warlock murmured. "Why should you speak the Royal Language of the Rigellians." As though the thought were more humorous than strange, he began to laugh in a cracked and bitter voice. Shana looked at her father fearfully, for it was obvious to her now that the Warlock was quite mad, and a mad demon was something much to be feared—perhaps even more than the warmen of Ulm and their Navigator.

"Can you help us, Lord?" asked Shevil.

"Perhaps, perhaps. Come see me tomorrow." The silver robe rustled as he prepared to step away, down the tunnel.

"Sire," Shana said carefully, "the warmen are *here*. Tomorrow we may all be dead."

The electronic eye clicked and hummed as the first moon began to break over the wooded ridges to the east.

"Sire? Please?" The girl's voice was soothing, gentle.

The Warlock rustled his robe irritably. "I am not a soldier. I'm not a weaponeer either—I am—" He stopped, a perplexed expression in his drug-blind eyes. "I am—" he began again. "Great Star, I don't *know* what I am, but I knew only a short while ago. While I slept, I knew." His voice grew agitated, tremulous with the beginnings of anger again. "How can I help you if I cannot help myself? Answer me that? Well, tell me, bird-girl. Tell me if you can."

Shevil said hopelessly, "You cannot arm us against the warmen?"

"Arm you? *Arm* you? Is that what you want? Is that all you think about, savage? Didn't I see you fighting against two of your own stinking kind only a moment ago? With a knife in your hand?" The voice rose again to that imperious pitch. *"I*

*am not a man into whose presence one may come armed! I
could have you killed for that!''*

Shevil hung his head, hope dead, beyond knowing what to
do now. The creature might be a demon, but if so, it was a
wildly insane demon and disinclined to help the folk in any
way.

*"You have a knife. Give it to me at once, or I shall call the
Guard!''*

Shevil looked dumbly at the knife he still held. It came to
the family from a demon place and now a demon demanded
its return. He extended it, hilt first. The Star and Spaceship
gleamed in the light from the fluoroglobes in the ceiling of the
tunnel. The Warlock's eye whispered and hummed.

"Rigell," the Warlock whispered, the lense fixed on the Imperial signet.

Memory battered against the synapses blocked by drug-
hunger. Rigell on the Star Throne. The Hall of Mirrors in
Nyor. Nyor—Queen of the Stars. Fragments of the past glittered like bits of broken crystal in Lord Ophir's mind.

Rigell was dead—long, long ago. *I am the Star King,* Ophir
thought. *I am the Galacton now.*

His eye searched the weathered faces of the man and the girl
before him. *These are my people.* He raised the lense to en-
compass the darkening sky dusted with the milky glow of the
galactic lens and the sliver of the first moon. He remembered
such a sky, on the world where he was born. The name? What
was the *name*? A Rimworld, where there were few visible
stars. A world of a star-system near the edge of the galaxy, far
from Nyor, farther still from the blazing skies of the crowded
Inner Marches.

"Lord—" Shevil released the knife-that-burns and let the
old demon hold it.

"I am trying to *remember* . . ."

"Yes, lord, but the *warmen*—" Shevil felt Shana's cautioning touch on his forearm.

"He will help us," the girl whispered.

"I am the Galacton!" The old man shrieked suddenly. The
eye fixed once again on Shevil Lar, and the voice firmed and
took on that deep regal timbre. "I *rule*."

"Of course, Lord. In this valley—"

"*Everywhere.*"

Shevil fell silent and whispered to himself a prayer that Shevaughn had taught him: *Blessed are the mad, for theirs is the kingdom of the heavens.*

"There are invaders in the valley, you say?"

"Yes, Lord," Shevil said hopelessly.

"Then you must bring my people here, to me. We will shelter them here until the legions arrive. The penalty for unlawful war is terrible death." The eye moved very close to Shevil and he struggled to bear the scrutiny without flinching. "Do I know you?" the old man asked. "The girl I recognize. She is my falconer. But who are you?"

"I am Shevil, Lord. Shevil Lar of Trama."

"Title? Your title, man! Quickly!"

Shevil looked at Shana helplessly.

"He is Duke of this place, Lord," Shana said, remembering the old title.

"Well, then, Duke Shevil," Ophir said grandly. "Bring your folk to me. The Star King is father to his people. We will shelter here."

"In the mountain?" Shevil asked. "They will not come, Lord. They will be afraid."

"This girl has been in the mountain," Ophir said, dismissing the objection. "There is nothing to fear."

"You know that, father," Shana said.

"But my daughter is an adept," Shevil said. "She is called a witch. The people will not heed her."

The Warlock said sternly, "If you are Duke of this place, *order* them to shelter with me. If they will not, let them face the rebels alone. The Galacton will defend his holding." With that, he turned and moved down the corridor, his robe extinguishing the lights behind him, one by one.

Shevil said desperately, *"They will not do it, Shana."*

"We must try to make them do it, father," the girl said quietly. "Is there another way?"

"Shana," Shevil Lar said, "I don't think he is a warlock or a demon. I think he is a mad old man. Nothing he says makes sense."

The girl held her father's arm and said with a wisdom far beyond her years, "Whatever he is, Shevil, he offers us more than Ulm's soldiers."

With deep misgivings, taking his daughter's hand, Shevil Lar picked his way between the still guttering, discarded torches down the mountain toward the dark houses where his people trembled in fear—caught between the madness of the Warlock and the lances of the warriors waiting for dawn on the ridge.

Chapter Seven

Historians of the Inner Planets have had, for many years, a tendency to regard the Rhad as simply a troublesome and warlike people, given to periodically disturbing the peace of the galaxy. This is an oversimplification of the Rhadan role in stellar politics. While it is true that during the Interregnal and Early Second Empire periods Rhadan warbands ravaged the Rimworlds with unparalleled ferocity, it is also true that the men of Rhada were among the first to support the standards of Glamiss during the Reconquest. And chroniclers of the First Empire record that Rhada, though far from the seat of Imperium at Nyor (on Sol III), was traditionally the personal holding of the King-Elector—the Heir to the Star Throne of the First Empire Galactons.

—Vikus Bel Cyb-1009, *Rhadan Influences in Galactic History*, Early Confederate period

Though I am not Rhadan by birth, I take pride in my Imperial Principate of that place. It is fitting that this

world of warriors should always be the hereditary holding of the man chosen Heir to the Imperium.

> —From a letter written by Fremir ibn Sol
> alt Messier (Rigell XXV) and discovered
> in the Imperial Archive of Nyor during
> the Late Second Stellar Empire period

Through the deepest part of the night, those hours when
both moons were in the sky, Glamiss watched the valley
through his monocular. He noted the torches and the gathering at the valley's far end, but even through the instrument, it
was impossible to make out clearly what the people of Trama
were doing in the distant moraine. First there was a gathering,
and then, much later, he could make out a few figures moving
up the moraine in the cold moonlight—but how many, and to
what purpose, he could not be certain.

In the fifth standard hour of the night, Warman Quant
relieved him at the watch, and Glamiss returned to the bivouac
to roll himself in his furred cloak and sleep for the time remaining until dawn.

The sky was filled with the bluish promise of sunrise when
Vulk Asa woke him. The eyeless face looked smooth as stone
in the shadowless skyglow.

"Glamiss Warleader, I have dreamed of Rahel," the Vulk
said.

Glamiss waited, wise in the ways of the Vulk. Asa's dream
might be simply one of the mildly prescient dreams the Vulk
frequently had (and which often provided intelligence of coming events that a clever warman would be advised to heed)—or
the dream might not be a dream at all, as humans understood
the term, but a sleep-waking contact with another Vulk, usually stronger and clearer than the mind-touch contacts forced
by the daylight necessities of the Vulks' masters.

"She is well?" Glamiss inquired, as manners dictated.

"Well enough, Warleader," the Vulk said with equal courtesy. Glamiss, though accustomed to these elliptical Vulkish
conversations, suppressed a certain impatience. Rahel, as the
more sensitive of the two Vulk owned by the House of Vara-
Vyka, was always kept confined in whatever keep Lord Ulm

was using to house his people. Glamiss considered this summary deprivation of liberty an unnecessary cruelty, but it was common practice among the lords of the various planets in this part of the Great Sky.

"She delivered your message to the Lord Ulm, of course."

"May she be thanked. But? There's a 'but' of some sort in your manner, Asa."

"The Lord Ulm refuses to send more men, Glamiss Warleader. He declares that fifty are more than enough to punish a village of weyrherders."

Glamiss frowned. He had not really expected Ulm to respond favorably to his request, but neither had he expected a flat refusal. Ulm, for all his bravado and bombast, was a compromising man. It had cost him lands and power on Vyka.

The Vulk waited.

"Was there something else, Vulk Asa?" Glamiss asked in a hard and angry voice.

"Rahel says that what the Lord Ulm says is not what the Lord Ulm intends. She says that the Bishop-Navigator Kaifa arrived at Vara with the starship *Gloria in Coelis* during the night—"

Glamiss frowned. "So soon? Emeric said—" He broke off and stared appraisingly down the slope to where Emeric the Rhadan was packing his kit and strapping on his weapons among the warmen. A faint suspicion struggled against his trust and affection for the Navigator. Were the Navigators playing with him? Were there plots within plots here? The Order's ways were often devious, sometimes even treacherous.

"There is more, Glamiss Warleader."

Glamiss looked at the Vulk's face. Like a smooth stone, he thought, an ageless, immutable permanence lived in that face. He shivered slightly and made the sign of the Star on his palate with his tongue. "Say on, Vulka Asa. What more is there?"

"This morning the warband's horses were loaded aboard the *Gloria*, together with war machines. She believes the men will go aboard soon with Lord Ulm, the Bishop, and the two Inquisitors who came with him from Aurora."

Glamiss felt the prickling warning of threatened disaster. "How do you read this, Asa?"

The Vulk turned slightly toward Nav Emeric, who was

strapping his mailed shirt now, arming himself. "Wouldn't you prefer to discuss this with the lord Nav Emeric?"

Glamiss's eyes narrowed. "I would not. I asked you a question. Answer it, Vulk."

Asa inclined his head. "My sister-wife, she-who-shares-with-me, and I believe that we were sent into this valley as a diversion, Glamiss Warleader. The Inquisition knows more of the strangeness here than you believe—"

"And Emeric?" Glamiss asked harshly.

"The lord Navigator is as innocent as I, Warleader. His order does not share all things with all its members."

"Can I believe that?"

"Yes, you can believe it. The Bishop has known of the witchcraft in Trama for a long time—or so Rahel thinks. The plan to use Ulm's warband to cleanse the valley comes from Algol, from the Grand Master Talvas, himself."

"Then why was I sent here with a small force?" Glamiss demanded.

"You are young, Glamiss," the Vulk said, "but you know the ways of the world. The answer is in your mind. I see it there."

"Ulm wants me dead."

"Yes, Warleader."

"He daren't risk a simple dagger or a challenge—"

The Vulk smiled thinly. "You are too popular with the warband for that. He will tell the soldiers that you have turned rebel—that you are bewitched by the dark powers in Trama. The Bishop-Navigator will support him—in exchange for a free hand for the Inquisition in this place."

"Well now," Glamiss said, holding his heavy Vykan sword thoughtfully. "I have come up in the world, Vulk Asa. Who would have thought a poor herdsman's son would rate a plot for his execution? With the connivance of the holy Order, at that."

Emeric, overhearing, stood at his shoulder. "What's this about executions, Glamiss? And the Order?"

Glamiss fixed his friend with a cold stare. "It seems you are expendible, Nav Emeric, for all that you're a noble of the Northern Rhad. Ulm is embarking the warband on the *Gloria* —but not exactly to come to our assistance here. He's weeded out the troopers loyal to me for this foray, and now he's coming with the warband to kill us. With the aid and blessing of the holy Order, friend priest. What do you make of that?''

Disbelief flashed in Emeric's eyes—and faded. There were, he realized, two faces to the Order of Navigators. One was theological, compassionate, concerned with the saving of the ancient treasures and men's souls. The other was simply expedient. What Glamiss said was quite possible—even understandable, if the rumors about witchcraft in Trama were true. The Inquisition sought to wipe out the black arts root and branch, true. But what the Inquisition burned out of the laity often found its way into the laboratories of Algol. The Order could be a stern father, cautioning all men in the Great Sky to "do as I say, not as I do."

Emeric raised his eyes to Vyka's first rim, now breaking through the mists of early morning along the treeline. He murmured an Ave Stella. Again, he thought, faith is challenged.

"I cannot believe that the Order is condoning treachery, Glamiss. But if Ulm is outlawing you, it is possible the *Gloria* might be put at his disposal. Ulm is your lord. Just or unjust, he has the right."

"No longer, Emeric. I say this to you and you must take it as a man, not as a priest. We will settle the right and wrong of this business when I hold Trama." The young warleader's eyes were narrowed against the dawn. He looked calculating, Emeric thought, more ruthless than one would have imagined possible in one so youthful.

Glamiss said, "Last night we spoke of Nyor. Those were dreams. Here's Trama. It is only a valley and a tribe of weyrherders and perhaps''— he smiled grimly —"some useful witchery. It is a fall, my friend priest, from the feathered cape of the Star King to shaggy weyr skins—but we'd best take what the time and place offer. I want to be in full command here before Ulm and your bishop can reach us." He shouted for the troop to mount, and turned again to Emeric. His tone was ironic, for he had controlled his anger now. "Who knows? It may be that future history will say something important happened here today."

Vulk Asa said softly, "Those who survive to write the history will decide that, Warleader."

*　　*　　*

The starship *Gloria in Coelis*, grounded on the sandy plain to the west of Lord Ulm of Vara's keep, was ancient. Though the men who presently flew her were the wisest of their time, they had no really clear notion of how the vessel operated, when it was built or how fast it traveled. From time out of mind, the Order of Navigators had trained its priests in the techniques of automated starflight by *rote*. Even now, as the *Gloria*'s two million metric tons depressed the soil of the Varan plain, the duty Navigators on the starship's bridge, were chanting the Te Deum Stella, the Litany for Preflight, this ritual being one of the first taught to young novice Navigators on the cloister-planets of Algol.

Though the three junior priests on the bridge were chanting the voice commands that activated the immense ship's systems, in fact only the propulsion units (sealed after manufacture in the time of the Empire) responded. The priests did not know that the vessel's life-support systems and its many amenities had ceased to function more than a thousand years earlier. The interior of the starship was lit by torches burning in wall-sconces, water and food were stored aboard in wooden casks, and the ship's atmosphere was replenished not by the scrubber units, as originally intended, but by the air that was taken aboard through the open ports and hatchways. The starships were capable of almost infinite range, for the engines operated on solar-phoenix units. But the length of any star voyage was limited by the food and water supply and by the fouling of the air by the hundreds of men and horses of the warbands the starships most often carried.

The bridge had been depolarized, and from within this consecrated area where only a Navigator might pass, the duty crew could see the squat towers and thick walls of Lord Ulm's keep. The warband, almost a thousand armed men, was mustering on the plain below the north tower, preparing to file into the vaulted caverns within the kilometer-long ship.

Brother Anselm, a novice who spoke with the heavy Slavic accents of the Pleiades Region, had the Conn. This honor was a small one, for the ship was not under way, but the engine cores were still humming from the recent voyage from Aurora, and Anselm, a fervent young man, imagined that the voice of the Holy Star was in them—and speaking directly to him.

He half-closed his eyes and chanted, "Planetary Mass two-third nullified and cores engaged for atmospheric flight at minus thirty and counting."

Brother Gwill, a thinly made and sour young Altairi, made the response, pressing the glowing computer controls in the prescribed sequence. "Cores One and Three at Energy Point Three, for the Glory of Heaven. Cores Two, Four, and Five coming into phase as the Lord of the Great Sky Commands."

"Hallelujah, Core Energy rising on scan curve," Anselm declared with fervid devotion.

Gwill glanced across the power console at Brother Collis, a slender and delicately made aristocrat from the Inner Planets. His look conveyed a great weariness with Anselm's holier-than-we attitude. At the moment, Collis (who would be ordained a full Navigator within the year) was standing by the Support Console, ready to play his part in the ritual, though the Support Console never came to life as the Power Console did. Nevertheless, pushing the inert and lightless studs on the support systems' racks was included in the Te Deum Stella and so the act was invariably performed, "For the Glory of the Star and the Holy Spirit."

"Null-grav power to main buss at Energy Point Five in the Name of the Holy Name."

"Null-gee to main buss at my hack, if it is pleasing to the Spirit," Gwill responded. In spite of himself he could not suppress a shiver of anticipation. At Energy Point Five, the power of the cores was fed into the lifting system and the vast starship would begin to lose mass. The tonnage that interacted with planetary gravity to give the ship its great weight when at rest would begin to dissipate into a spatio-temporal anomaly, changing the molecular structure by reversing the atomic polarities of all matter within the Core field. The men who designed and built the starships understood this effect only imperfectly, and the Navigators who now flew them across the Great Sky understood it not at all. But the visual and physical effects of the change in matter within the Core fields was spectacular and awesome. As the Null-grav buss was activated, the skin of the ship would begin to shimmer and glow, surplus

energy accumulated by kinesis and radiation from the Vyka
Sun expending itself as light and molecular motion until the
starship actually began to move. It was a sight that created
consternation among the common folk of all the Great Sky,
and even Navigators, who were accustomed to the phe-
nomena, gave thought to the miraculous and holy nature of
the great ships that were their domain.

Anselm murmured to Brother Collis, "Gloria in Excelsis,
let the ship's pressure rise to ambient."

"Ambient it is and blessed be the Holy Star," Collins said
rapidly. He pressed the prescribed buttons on the Support
Console and waited the required thirty heartbeats. Nothing
happened, nor did the young novice expect anything to happen. The display screen remained dark. "We are hold, hold,
hold, may it be pleasing to God," he reported in the familiar
rising chant. "Hold on pressure, hold on flow, hold on
storage."

At this point in the Litany came the bitter indictment of Sin
and Cyb, who were the Adversaries of all that was good, as
well as of man in space. Collis often considered the possibility
that this part of the ritual had not come from the Holy Books
of Starflight enshrined in Algol, but had been added to the
Litany in the dim past to explain why the Support Console
always remained inert.

The three priests made the sign of the Star and Anselm indicated that Brother Gwill should make the Query.

The novice punched in the coded sequence that was one of
the first things memorized by all Navigators and meant, in effect, "Are we where we should be?" Ordinarily, for a short atmospheric flight, the Query was omitted from the Litany, but
nothing was *ever* left out when Brother Anselm was in charge
of the countdown.

The ship's computer flashed its reply on the display-screen:
"*Position coordinates D788990658-RA008239657. Province
of Vega, Area 10, Aldrin. Planetary coordinates 23° 17' north
latitude, 31° 12' west longitude. Inertial navigation system
engaged.*"

In spite of their familiarity with the ways of the holy starships, the three novices felt a tingling thrill at the appearance
of the strangely shaped sigils in the ancient Anglic runes of the

Empire. They had only the vaguest notion of what the ship meant by addressing them in these mystical words, in these phrases of the ancient world. But the background color on the display screen was the Color of Go—emerald green—and that told them that the *Gloria in Coelis* was, once again, ready for flight.

In the Great Hall of the *Gloria,* Bishop-Navigator Kaifa, a rock-faced, dour man in the customary homespun habit and mailed shirt of the Order, sat at a table with Lord Ulm and his lieutenants—three middle-aged warriors in animal-skins and plate-and-leather armor.

Ulm was a gross man, heavy in the jowls, his black beard shot with gray. He wore his armor and weapons with difficulty on his corpulent body and his breathing wheezed. Kaifa, eyeing him critically, guessed that he suffered from dropsy—his naked legs and ankles were puffy and swollen and one could see the laboring heartbeat in his throat. Ulm would probably be dead before the next season-change, Kaifa thought coldly, and small loss it would be for the people of his holding. But when Ulm was dead, who would take his place, the Bishop wondered. Which of the hungry-eyed captains here would swing the heavier sword and win the overlordship of Vara? Whatever Ulm's shortcomings as a man and ruler, he was—if not devout—at least properly afraid of the clergy. Whoever came to rule in this part of Aldrin (the Bishop used, in his mind, the ancient name for the planet because to him *Vyka* encompassed the entire star system with its three habitable worlds) must submit to the guidance of the Order of Navigators because the planet was a political nexus. The computers in Algol had made it clear for many years that the valley of Trama on Aldrin was psychopolitically vital to the next stage of development for man in space.

Many of the elders of the Order disputed the truths obtained from the Algol computers—declaring them to be the work of Sin and Cyb. Kaifa smiled contemptuously. The Order, like the works of man everywhere, was slipping into barbarism—losing touch with the scientific realities. It was the mission of men like himself, he thought with fanatic fervor, to stop and reverse this trend. If innocents had to go to the burning stakes of the Inquisition, it was a pity. But the old knowledge was best held by those who could use it for the eventual benefit of all men—and the end justified any means, however brutal.

"It is understood, my lord Ulm," Kaifa said, "that the valley of Trama *and all it may contain* becomes a holding of the Order. Under your suzerainty, of course, but holy ground."

Ulm bridled slightly, his ruddy face showing displeasure at the thought of surrendering any of his lands to the Navigators. But it was the warman Linne who repeated the locals' objections. "The people belong to the lord, Nav Kaifa. It has always been so and I don't see what there is so special about the place that requires a change in our ancient customs. if there's Sin and Cyb there, we'll burn whoever you say. But giving up the valley—" He scowled his disagreement and looked impatiently at his lord.

Ulm said heavily, "What Linne says is true, Bishop. I think the Order's price is too high."

Kaif's eyes glittered coldly. "Lord Ulm, you had better consider carefully. I am placing my ship at your disposal. You have sent one of your own people into the valley, knowing there is no escape except over the mountains. You say Glamiss is disloyal—very well. I have seen no evidence of this, you understand, but if it is your wish to accuse him and kill him in that place, it is no concern of mine. But there is a Navigator with him—a noble Rhad. Your need to eliminate a popular captain may cost the Order the life of one of its best young priests. You must recompense us for this."

Linne spoke. (Will it be Linne? Kaifa wondered. Is he the one?) The warman's voice was harshly scornful. "How many soldiers are *you* contributing, Lord Bishop?"

Kaifa fixed the captain with an iron stare. "None. Not one." He spoke quietly, with a deadly calm. "But look about you, Linne." He indicated the great, dark-vaulted chamber in which they met. The upper reaches of the curving, groined overhead were lost in shadow. The flambeaux fixed to the walls could not illuminate the cavernous interior of the great ship's salon. "Think where you are, warleader. This is a holy place—" all made the sign of the Star. "Yes, I see you understand that. Without the starships, what will become of Vara?

In a season you will be without weapons and armor. In two you will be hungry. In three, you will be living in caves like naked savages. It is the holy starships that sustain men, Linne Warleader, and the Order of Navigators controls the starships."

A heavy silence fell over the men at the table. Kaifa waited, his hands calmly folded under the homespun of his habit.

Linne chewed his lower lip sullenly. "What you say is true, holy father. But your price is high."

"The Order has no price, Linne," the Bishop said. "The Order *is*. What we do is not for *your* understanding."

Ulm shifted his bulk uncomfortably and said, "We accept that, my lord Bishop. It is only that—"

Kaifa held up his hand. "Decide, Ulm. And give the order to unload your men and horses if you wish."

Ulm's protuberant eyes showed his fear. "Would you excommunicate us, Bishop? Would you punish us for bargaining?"

Kaifa raised his cowl so that the warriors at the table could see the dread Red Fist of the Inquisition. "Do not make me doubt your devotion to the Star, Lord Ulm."

Ulm shuddered. He bowed his head. Kaifa turned his steady gaze to Linne and the other captains. They, too, broke under the threat. *The Order,* Kaifa thought exultantly, *the Order overbears them.*

He said, "Well. Decide. Now."

Ulm muttered, "We meant no disrespect, Bishop."

"The valley of Trama and all it contains?"

Ulm nodded.

"Bless you, my sons," the Bishop said, making the sign of the Star over them.

Ulm asked humbly, "But Glamiss and the men who turned against me?"

Bishop-Navigator Kaifa thought contemptuously: *Here is a lord of our time. A young mercenary is loved by his men and for this he must die—and they with him.* He thought for a moment about Emeric Aulus Kevin Kiersson-Rhad. If the Navigator was lost in this outworld skirmish between barbarians, there would be bitterness on Rhada and questions asked, perhaps by the Grand Master himself. That was a pity, but what must be, would be. The computer on Algol had said that whoever held Trama became a prime-mover. The *why* of it was, like so much else, lost in the jumble of mysticism and fear that attended the workings of those few ancient machines that remained operable.

Fact: Bishop-Navigator Kaifa knew, Trama is vital to the Order. *Fact:* Once cleared of inhabitants *and* Ulm's men, the valley could be examined, explored, and its mysteries unraveled by qualified members of the Order of Navigators. *Fact:* To obtain this freedom of search for the Order, a price must be paid—regrettably, in blood. The lives of the inhabitants, of the "punitive" expedition as well, were forfeit. And finally, it was also a fact that none of this could be accomplished without an alliance of the moment between the First Pilot and Commander of the holy vessel *Gloria in Coelis* and this gross and corpulent savage who sat wheezing fearfully before the austere Bishop. Glamiss, a promising young warrior, and Emeric of Rhada, an equally promising young priest-Navigator, were the price of it all. Kaifa sighed slowly and thought, *So be it and amen.*

He said, "We are finished here then, Lord Ulm. You will have a free hand against your Warleader Glamiss. The Order will occupy the valley of Trama." He rose to indicate that the audience was over. "When your troops have finished loading, send word to me and the *Gloria* will carry us to battle."

"As you command, holy father," wheezed Ulm.

Kaifa looked at Linne. The bearded warman nodded sulky agreement.

"Then peace be with you, my sons," the Navigator said, unconscious of any irony.

Chapter Eight

Given the existence of the Order of Navigators and the still-operable starships of the First Empire, there is no psychohistorical reason for the state of human society in the galaxy during the dark years of the Interregnum. It is true that the human population was widely dispersed, and that men had suffered a racial shock from the ferocity of the Civil Wars that destroyed the hegemony of the Rigellian Galactons. Still, the *means* of achieving unity existed. What was lacking was the *vision*. From the rabble of contending warlords on the worlds of the "Great Sky" it was necessary to develop one true *conqueror*. And such a man—the charismatic leader with a complete and unique purview of man's history did not yet exist.

> —Vikus Bel Cyb-1009, *The Origins of the Second Stellar Empire,* Early Confederate period

None knew that Rigell XXIX lived, preserved past his time by the hopeful cryonic techniques of the dying Empire. Or perhaps it would be more accurate to say that the *idea* of Rigell XXIX lived—for his world was dust.

> Ibid.

The Lord Ophir ben Rigell ibn Sol alt Messier regarded his sleep-tank with longing; his old body craved the maintenance dose of trilaudid that would send him back into his waking dream. For the first time that he could remember, he was aware of the opulence of his apartments in the hospital. It was a luxury to which he seemed to be accustomed. The drug still in his system illuminated fragments of memory: the suite he had occupied on the *Delos*, the quarters that had been his in the city between the two rivers, other tantalizing bits of recollection from his former life. Everything that filtered through his mind seemed accoutered with opulence, pomp, and great ceremony. And it was this, strangely, that now troubled Ophir and kept him from retreating still again into his drugged dreaming.

Elsewhere in the warren of corridors, operating theaters, and public rooms that comprised the main part of the hospital, he could hear the murmurous wonder of the people of Trama. Not all had taken refuge inside the mountain. The hetman had been unable to overcome the superstitious fears of many. But now fully fifty or more of the folk had followed him and his daughter into "The Warlock's Keep." Some, Ophir realized with fastidious distaste, had even brought their animals with them.

The confusion they were causing was distressing to the old man and yet he did not react as he had imagined he might—with imperious anger and disgust at their savage ways. Instead, he withheld indulgence in his own pleasures—the tank and trilaudid—aware that, in some way, he was personally responsible for the safety and well-being of these simple creatures.

Though Ophir's chemically damaged brain was only dimly aware of it, twenty-nine generations of imperial royalty had produced him. Despite a lifetime spent in self-indulgence and enjoyment of all the vices a moribund civilization could produce, those twenty-nine generations and the early training he had undergone to prepare him to rule an empire of a thousand suns affected him now. The last of the Rigellians was a captive of his own *noblesse*. He felt responsible.

With an effort, he forced himself to plan. Earlier, in a fit of anger, he had considered using the instruments remaining in the hospital as weapons against the barbarian soldiers about to invade his valley. A more rational appraisal of these possibilities presented him with innumerable problems. When he had entered the hospital for the Sleep, Aldrin had been a relatively peaceful world. The troubles on the rim of the galaxy were still decades and parsecs away. It was unlikely that Aldrin had become, at some later date, an outpost of empire. Ophir, in his best days, had been no soldier. But he, like all imperials, had been aware of the power available to the military. Atomics of a thousand, ten thousand, a *million* megatons were commonplace in the arsenal of the Imperial Fleet. Planet-smashers were simply a matter of a decision to build them, for thermonuclear weapons were open-ended.

But he had seen no sign of such destruction in the valley, and he had heard of no such catastrophes from the natives. They sometimes spoke, in their prayers to him, of "the time of falling suns," so there had been some sort of engagement on Aldrin. But it appeared to have been a small one, and at some distance from the hospital in the valley.

So there were no weapons as such nearby, Ophir thought painfully. His drug-hunger plagued him, but he persisted. Petulantly, it was true, he had invited the folk to take sanctuary. Or had he? Was it that half-naked girl or her father who had done it? No matter. The folk of the valley were crude—but they were peaceful. Except for their offer of human sacrifice and their disgusting habit of slaughtering weyr on his doorstep, they were not troublesome. The barbarian warband was quite another matter. Ophir had no intention of allowing a mob of spear-carrying human offal to destroy the repose of his last days. For he understood well enough now that he would die in the valley of Trama.

The pale green sky of Aldrin was the last he would ever see. His blind eyes leaked tears. Never to see Nyor again, never to walk through the gardens and avenues of the Queen of the Skies—Dihanna, he thought, never to ride with her across the windswept plains of Rhada and breathe the scent of her mingled with the cold tang of the Rhad land's seawind—

I would have taken you to my own holding, Dihanna, he thought with deep grief. *To my dark coasts and oceans of waving grass and skies gray and crossed with the lightning and the aurora—*

The memory flared into an unbearable poignancy, and he

felt the tingle of the permissive garment he wore touching him with the tiny steel tongues that fed him his beloved trilaudid.

"No," he said aloud. "Not now."

The hospital computer spoke through the speaker in his chamber. "It is time for your medication, sir."

"No," Ophir said again. "There is work to do."

The computer pondered this strange statement and found nothing in its programming to account for it. With mechanical stupidity, it said, "You are not strong enough to undergo withdrawal therapy, sir." Ophir's robe tingled again.

"Strong enough?" The Warlock gave a hysterical laugh. "You brainless machine—don't you know I'm dying?"

"We only wish to make you comfortable, sir," said the droning voice.

"Are there weapons here?" Ophir asked, ignoring the bland acceptance of encroaching death.

"That question is beyond my competency, sir. I am a medical computer," the voice said.

"You are *nothing*," the old man said with sudden fury. "You are an anachronism—*worthless*."

The computer, failing to detect a question, remained silent.

Ophir came to his feet with an effort. The weight of his prosthesis seemed too much to bear. His shoulder ached with it. He felt the torturing thirst and dermal sensitivity that warned of trilaudid withdrawal syndrome. He forced himself to ignore it and went into the passageway.

He had never been trained medically, but an imperial heir's education was catholic. A man destined to rule an empire dare not be a specialist. The thought was clouded and scarred with lacunae of amnesia, but the form of it was there. Ophir's sense of responsibility was forcing him to reaccept the realities he had abandoned so long ago in his hedonistic flight from a civilization he despised as corrupt.

The standard instruments to be found in a hospital of his time—the personality probes and exchangers, the hypno-teachers, the lasers and sonic scalpels—must exist in this echoing tomb, he thought vaguely. Perhaps he was engineer enough to use them as weapons? And if they were not effective agencies for destruction, surely they could be used to overawe a troop of savages?

He forced aching thoughts through his mind, examining and discarding. He could hear the weyrherders of Trama. They had gathered in one of the common rooms and were huddling there, praying to who knew what dark gods?

To you, Ophir beloved, the lady Dihanna whispered in his ear, *they are praying to you, their Prince.*

The holographic projectors from the library, Ophir thought suddenly. For a beginning, the ghostly warriors of the Dawn Age, created from the plays and novels of Earth before the Age of Space. Yes, he thought, suddenly gleeful: that for a beginning. But as an overture, as something to give the invaders a taste of terror—the eagles.

His cracked laughter rang down the vaulted corridor. *First the wild birds and then the shadowy hosts of Stalingrad, Agincourt, Bataan, and Kasserine. Why, one had the whole bloodsoaked history of man to choose from! When one had history, what need of soldiers?* The holographic projectors were easily portable—suddenly the whole pattern of the engagement to come took on the dimensions of a beautiful, cosmic joke. He laughed gleefully and trotted unsteadily toward the sound of his devotee's prayers. If it was magic they wanted, a Prince of the Rigellian Empire would give them magic.

Chapter Nine

With an heart of furious fancies
Whereof I am commander
With a burning spear and a horse of air
To the wilderness I wander.
By a knight of ghosts and shadows
I summoned am to tourney
Ten leagues beyond the wide world's end—
        —Fragment attributed to R.L. Stevenson,
         Dawn Age poet

   My ancestors were men of no sensitivity or imagination. It takes many generations to produce a truly *talented* man.
      —Torquas the Poet, Vykan
        Galacton of the Second Empire, Middle
        Second Stellar Empire period

The morning sun was marking its path along the western cliff faces of the valley of Trama as Glamiss led his company down the steep path into the treeline.

A stillness lay on the valley. The wind was down and the

sound of the river came softly through the forest. Occasionally a mare would mutter or a padded foot would bring a sound from the shale of the path. The warmen studied the sky, wary of the eagles.

At the foot of the shale talus where the ground leveled and sloped more gently toward the meadows, Glamiss signaled the flank guards out. Three horsemen on each side vanished into the thickening brush growing among the tree trunks.

From their packs the warmen had taken crossbows, stubby machines with curling pistol grips and twin horn-bows cocked by the small windlass at the butt end of the weapon. The crossbows were each loaded with two quarrels of lead or shaped stone affixed to a leather tail to hold the missles straight in flight.

The crossbows were not favored weapons among the horseback soldiers, who preferred their short throwing lances and the heavy swords sheathed at their backs. But Glamiss was a strict disciplinarian, and his men learned the use of the crossbow or risked his displeasure—which could be severe.

Now the weapons were carried across the saddlebows, held in the left hand while the right held the throwing lances. The mares, of course, needed no guidance by their riders save the spoken or mental commands.

Glamiss had learned this particular selection of weaponry and technique on Rhada, while serving there in the household of some blood-kin of Emeric's during one of the infrequent intervals when Ulm enjoyed good relations with the Northern Rhad. Alone among the troops of Ulm of Vara were the men Glamiss had trained in this fashion.

Riding at Glamiss's side, Emeric said, "It's too quiet by half. Where are those wild birds?"

Glamiss glanced at the high canopy of trees above their heads. "We will see them when we reach the open meadows."

Emeric, who as a priest-Navigator did not carry a throwing lance, swung the morningstars on the end of his flail anxiously. He was battlewise and experienced, as any Rhad would be and as all Navigators were as well, but he had never been able to cure himself of the habit of nervous talk before an engagement.

"Vulk Rahel could have been mistaken about Ulm," he

said. "The Order would never help him to attack his own
people."

"You are a man of faith, Nav Emeric," Glamiss said dryly.
"But Vulk Rahel was not mistaken. Matters have been touchy
between me and my bond-lord for some time. I am a threat to
him."

"Are you, Glamiss?" the Navigator asked.

"Yes, he's right to think of me so," Glamiss replied. "It
may shock your Rhad sense of honor, but the thought of taking Vara-Vyka from him has been in my mind more than
once."

Emeric rode in silence, listening to the soft clatter of
weapons behind them. Glamiss was right. It *did* offend his
Rhad sense of the fitness of things to think of his friend as a
possible oathbreaker and rebel. But against that one had to
weigh the savage way Ulm ran his fief, his cruelty to his
people, and the gradual deterioration of the holding under
Ulm's stewardship. Barbarism was like a lapping bog everywhere on the worlds of the Great Sky. The Order of Navigators could salvage and protect only so much of the civilization
of the old Empire. It could not accomplish the reversal of a
tide of savagery alone. What was needed, Emeric realized, was
a class of tough-minded, reasonably enlightened rulers for the
people—men who could think beyond the next meal, the next
wench, the next border raid. Men, when all was said, like
Glamiss the Vykan.

He thought again of the strange dream Glamiss had described last evening. His friend was no liar, Emeric thought
with a shiver, and no man would court the Adversaries by
spinning tales on the night before battle. Glamiss *had* dreamed
and *did* dream of Nyor, Queen of the Stars. What was it that
stimulated so hopeless, so strange a dream, Emeric wondered.
Was it some racial memory, some remembrance of man's days
of glory? Or was it the intercession of God in the Holy Star,
pointing a path toward—what?

That men must unite or perish was common knowledge
among the educated classes. But knowing something to be true
was an unbelievable distance from the reality. By what path,
then? The priest-Navigator looked ahead along the shaded
trail into the valley of Trama. *This* one? Was there something

here that transformed an outland skirmish—a bit of border-lord treachery—into a keystone of . . . Emeric's thoughts collapsed into a welter of unbelievable images: of great armies of warmen storming across the galaxy, a jihad of unification—bloody and terrible but essential if man were to survive among the holy stars, and at the end of the path—Glamiss, in the crown and feathered cape of the Star King, lord of an empire. An *Empire*?

The priest shook his head, shaken by his visions. What am I thinking? Glamiss is a fine soldier, but he is only a man. To recreate what was once a hegemony encompassing a thousand suns needed more than a man. It needed a hero with a clear vision of all that had ever been—and all that might one day *be*.

Emeric glanced at his friend's intent face under the rim of his iron helmet. *I do not wish this for you, Glamiss,* he thought. *I love you as a brother, and I pray that this dream will pass from you . . .*

"*Eagles!*" A flanker was galloping toward the column from the left, where the forest was thinning into grassland and river bank. Emeric heard the high-pitched scream of the great birds and saw shadows crossing the sun above the canopy of trees.

Glamiss rose in the stirrups and gave a sharp command. The troop wheeled toward the open ground, the mares snarling angrily.

"Emeric, stay with Asa," Glamiss said.

"I don't plan to miss this fight," the Navigator said.

Glamiss smiled grimly. "I didn't think you did. But you have no crossbow and I need someone to protect the Vulk."

Emeric frowned but accepted the mild rebuff. As a priest-Navigator he was, technically, under no one's commands but his superiors in the clergy. But, practically, priests serving as military chaplains took their orders from the warleaders in tactical charge of operations. In war, the warband must survive and, if possible, triumph. The niceties of protocol submitted to the needs of the battle.

He wheeled Sea Wind and trotted to the rear where Vulk Asa sat perched on the broad back of an over-age but still pugnacious war mare.

"The eagles are definitely under mental control now," the Vulk said, his smooth face lifted skyward. "The controller is a human adept. A young female."

Emeric made the sign of the Star and gripped the handle of his flail more firmly. "How would a peasant girl learn such things, Asa?" he wondered aloud.

"How, indeed, Nav Emeric. There is much that is strange in this valley," the Vulk replied.

Emeric watched the warband's movements at the edge of the forest. Glamiss had dispersed the troopers at the treeline and they waited there, under cover of the high canopy of leaves, while the flank guards circled out into the open meadow beyond.

As the eagles caught sight of the mounted men in the open they took up a screaming clamor, wheeling and beating the clear mountain air with their great pinions to gain altitude for their first attacks.

Emeric watched them with a feeling of apprehension. These birds had been used for blood sports in the time of the Empire, but they had bred in the wild in this place, and so were far more savage than the "falcons" used by imperial nobles to bring down mountain game. He wondered at the degree of control being exercised on them by the unknown falconer. In the last years of the Golden Age, telepathic control of birds and animals had been commonplace. The holy emanations of the stars, the hard radiations pouring from the great solar phoenixes, had caused millions of human and animal mutations in the early days of galactic travel, and applied genetics had produced not only strains of mentally receptive beasts, but a class of human adepts to control them.

Even now, after the dark confusion of the Interregnum's unnumbered centuries, the results of these trends survived. The Rhadan mare between his knees was a descendant of animals bred from the stock of mythic Earth to understand and respond to the energies generated by the human brain.

But here in Trama, Emeric thought, the remnants of the Empire seemed stronger, more fully preserved—and somehow more terrifyingly hostile.

He looked again at Glamiss, in his element now, controlling his men with gestures and signals. Yes, the Navigator thought, it was easy to see why a gross and abusive dullard like Lord Ulm would fear Glamiss and want him dead. The warmen responded to the young leader with a spirit and élan that were rare among the troops of the savage lands.

In the meadow, the flankers had formed a skirmishing circle, cantering in seemingly random patterns, always moving, tempting the eagles to attack.

"The adept is no soldier," Vulk Asa said. "Look, now."

The birds milled and screamed a hundred meters in the air. Emeric, unfamiliar with the tactics of attack from the air as he was, sensed that they were bunching, and that this was wrong. Had the adept been himself, he thought (with a Navigator's scholastic mind), he would have divided the birds and attacked the skirmishers on the flanks, forcing them to abandon their cantering mobility. Instead, the eagles swooped together in a shrieking, thrumming mass. The Navigator swallowed hard. There were fully a hundred birds in the feathered, clawed cloud diving at the horsemen—possibly the entire eagle population of the valley.

As the larger and swifter birds outdove their companions, the horsemen wheeled and galloped for the treeline. Their crossbows and lances were held ready, but not used. Instead, the skirmishers were drawing the birds toward the trees, luring them to a level below the high canopy and into the forest.

The riders approached the standing troop at an extended run, the birds close behind them, claws and beaks extended. Emeric wet his lips and held more tightly to the handle of his flail. The eagles were magnificent—and terrifying. Their great wings made a thrumming noise in the forest and their shrieking pierced the brain.

The skirmishers poured through the open ranks of the troopers and into the forest to turn in a wide circle and return. Meanwhile, Glamiss had given a shouted command and there was a noise like the sound of fifty great lute-strings being plucked. A flight of metal quarrels converged on the low-flying eagles, striking home with a terrible thudding patter.

A dozen birds were torn apart in flight by the heavy missiles. The pale grasses of the meadow were suddenly spattered with dark blood.

Vulk Asa averted his face and moaned as his sensitive, non-human mind staggered under the death-thoughts of the mutilated eagles.

Glamiss gave a command and the crossbows were fired
again, their second strings loosing a final barrage of quarrels.
A half-dozen birds tumbled to the ground. The meadow
seemed to boil with dying, wounded eagles. The remainder
fluttered and screamed, beating at the air with frantic
fury—some seeking to escape to higher altitudes, others still
raging to reach the horsemen sheltering under the feathery
trees.

Some few of the birds had flown into the forest and crashed
heavily into the palisade of tree trunks, stunning themselves or
injuring their wings. Emeric caught sight of a shimmering
brown body hurtling downward toward Vulk Asa who sat
defenseless and unaware on his growling mare. The animal
reared and bared her claws to meet the attack. In the confined
space between the trees, Emeric wheeled his mount and swung
his morningstars in a sweeping arc above the Vulk's head. The
spiked balls crushed the eagle's chest, and the great bird
tumbled to the leafy floor of the forest to lie gasping, talons
extended in final defiance. Emeric looked at the iridescent
feathers and bright blood, sickened by the cruel death of a
magnificent creature.

The Vulk spoke thinly, as though from a great distance.
"The adept is weeping," he said. "She feels the death of the
birds."

At the forest's edge, Glamiss had reformed the troop into a
single rank and at a command the men moved out into the
meadow, throwing lances ready. The birds had scattered, but
some few, who were too low to fly over the treetops without
making a heavy circle, were forced to fly across the warband's
front. A volley of thrown spears took a further bloody toll
from the eagles. Another score fell, pierced by the iron-tipped
javelins.

"They flee, Warleader!" a trooper shouted with shrill excitement. He wheeled to break ranks and pursue the flight,
sword drawn in futile threat.

"Thesu! Back into ranks!" Glamiss shouted warningly.

It was too late for the man who had broken the warband's
iron discipline. From low above the canopy of leaves a large
bird appeared in a shrieking dive. Emeric watched in horror as
the eagle's talons struck the warman's unprotected throat,

dragged him from his mare, and left him crumpled, spilling his life onto the grass to mingle with the blood of the slaughtered birds.

Thesu's mare screamed in rage and grief for her master, rearing to reach hopelessly for the vanishing eagles.

A stillness fell on the meadow. Emeric was amazed to realize that the entire engagement had taken no more than the space of five hundred heartbeats.

Despite the urgency of the need to move quickly across the valley, Glamiss took the time required for Emeric to say the ancient prayers for the dead over the body of the foolish Thesu. The Navigator noted that the men approved of this, and he noted, too, the sincere grief on the face of the young warleader. As he prayed over Thesu, he could not help but think of the future he and Glamiss had been discussing earlier. If Glamiss were indeed the conqueror to be, how many times would this scene be repeated? A thousand times a thousand, for though the worlds of the Great Sky lay supine and ready for conquest, a jihad would bleed the galaxy white before it was done.

At a command from Glamiss, the troop loaded the body of the dead warman on his mare, who moaned her sorrow, and placed her at the rear of the column with Vulk Asa. Then the band moved out again, crossing the meadows toward the river.

Once again, Glamiss dispatched outriders to scout ahead and led the troop along the riverbank in the directions of the clutch of hovels that lay under the far loom of the mountains.

In the distance, Emeric could see the soaring shapes of eagles, but the birds stayed high and far off, as though the adept who controlled them had been shocked into despair by the savagery of the Vara-Vykans' counterattack and could not bring herself to press home another costly foray.

The bright morning was growing slightly warmer as the rays of the Vyka sun touched the lower levels of the western cliffs. Here and there the meadows and the thinning groves of conifers were in sunlight. Emeric said to Glamiss, "It is a beautiful valley, Glamiss Warleader."

"The sky is filled with beautiful places—and ugly men,"

Glamiss replied bitterly, his heart heavy with the death of his trooper.

The warband moved silently, for on the soft riparian ground the mares' padded feet made no sound at all. The stillness was palpable, and Emeric listened to it as he would have listened to a whisper.

"Where have the people gone?" he wondered aloud.

Glamiss did not reply, though he was wondering the same thing. Moving steadily along the riverbank, the troop was swiftly approaching the village. But there was no movement in the place. The mill dominating the ford in the river was deserted; the waterwheel turned, and Glamiss could see the paddles rising, dripping diamond bright in the morning sun. But there was no sound and no sign of human habitation.

Beyond the hovels, the warleader could now see the path that appeared to lead upward toward the moraine and the glacier shining ice-blue on the slope of the mountains.

He raised his monocular and studied the rocky, rising ground. He estimated the distance at no more than two or three kilometers, and in the brilliant light the rocks and shadows were sharply limned in the glass. Farther up the slope he noted what appeared to be a platform of dressed stone or ferroconcrete. He felt a tingle of excitement as he realized that he was looking at a remnant of some ancient imperial construction. The stonemasons of Vara—in fact, of Vyka or any other planet of the Great Sky—could produce no such architecture.

He handed the glass to the Navigator riding at his side and said, "Under the glacier. What do you think of it?"

Emeric studied the concrete platform, noting the broad steps and what appeared to be the Anglic inscription on the archway. His heart began to beat more swiftly. "It's imperial. No doubt of it."

Glamiss smiled grimly. "The lair of your warlock, no doubt."

Emeric continued to study the construction. He could not read the inscription at this distance clearly, but it seemed to contain the word "hospital," and if his memory of the ideographs was accurate, the word "cryonic," which was almost meaningless to him, for he understood the concept only as

"colder-than-possible," which was but one of the many paradoxes inherent in the language of the men of the Golden Age.

Suddenly his breath quickened. As he watched, human figures seemed to materialize out of the mountain. All but one
were simply skin-clad natives of the valley (explaining where
the people had gone, it seemed). They were carrying a number
of machines of unholy and sinful appearance and placing
them on the concrete platform. Emeric made the sign of the
Star as he caught the glitter of metal and glass. But it was the
figure directing the operations that turned his blood to water.
For it must be the Warlock himself. There could be no other
explanation for the creature's singular appearance: dressed in
a robe of shimmering silvery metal that appeared flamelike at
this distance, bareheaded so that one could see the very ordinary white hair of an old man. But on the Warlock's shoulder
rode a familiar of shining metal with a single, great eye of
glass that gleamed in the sunlight.

"Glamiss. Look."

The warleader took the glass and his lips tightened into a
hard line. "Is it a man, priest?" he asked.

Emeric wondered at the cold calmness in his friend's voice.
Even a priest, who like himself had been carefully educated to
accept the dark wonders of the past, might well be stricken
with terror at the look of the apparition directing the activity
on the mountain. Yet Glamiss remained unmoved and unin-
timidated.

"A man, I think," Emeric said. "The sorcerer of Trama,
most probably. See how afraid of him the others are."

"It's the business of peasants to be afraid," Glamiss said.
"What I want to know is, can he harm us? What are those
machines they are emplacing?"

Emeric shrugged despairingly, filled with a sense of his own
and his Order's inadequacy in the presence of the ancient
science.

"I don't know, Glamiss," he admitted.

"Are they weapons?"

"I don't know that, either, Glamiss."

"They don't appear to be," the warman said slowly. "But
I've heard of machines that once threw firebolts."

The priest made the sign of the Star. "Energy weapons have

all been rendered harmless by God in the Star, Glamiss Warleader—'' This was a basic tenet of Navigator dogma. The Star had brought low not only the sinful men of the Golden Age, but he had also destroyed the weapons they used to break civilization down. It was one of the first things taught in the cloister worlds of Algol. But was it true—? The sinfulness of the thought was staggering. A Navigator must not doubt, ever. Still—

Glamiss said dryly, "I hope that the creature up there on the mountain has gotten the word of the Star in this matter, Emeric. Those machines look like projectors."

Emeric remembered the fragmentary carvings and crystal solideographs he had seen among the treasures of the Order in Algol—pictures of Sin and Cyb killing men in war. Some were battle scenes from the distant Dawn Age, and the weapons were familiar, for they were essentially those used by men now. But others were of the wars of expansion fought by the men of the Empire, and in these the weapons were often energy-based: laserifles, killer beams, and bolt-guns—the very stuff of Sin and Cyb, for in those days the Adversaries were gaining strength for their final, terrible assault on the children of the Star.

"It cannot be, Glamiss. There are no usable energy weapons in all the Great Sky, nor anyone who knows how they are made," he said with more conviction than he felt.

Glamiss lowered his glass and searched the deserted banks of the river. "Let us hope that your Warlock is as convinced of this as the Order," he said.

"Amen to that," muttered the priest.

Glamiss gave a hand signal, and the troop moved into extended order as they approached the ford. Across the river the mill, looking as though it had been hastily abandoned, seemed to stare at the soldiers from blank-eyed windows. Beyond it, among the few hovels of the village, a pariah-dog, its red tongue lolling, loped among the village litter. No other sound broke the morning stillness and Emeric could hear the soft lapping of the paddles in the millrace.

Warman Quant, riding just behind Emeric and the warleader, mumbled an audible prayer. Emeric turned in time to see several others making witchsigns and he felt a pang of exasperation mixing with his apprehension. How were men ever to pull themselves out of this endless barbarism, laden down as they were with all the superstitions a thousand or more years of darkness could produce?

Even the ritual of his own Order, thought the Navigator, was so filled with signs and sigils that a man couldn't tell what was the true knowledge of the ancients and what was pure warlockry. The Chinese of fabled Earth were said, however, to have had a proverb: *The longest journey begins with a single step.* To bring the race back to the height it had once scaled, to unite the men of the thousand suns again, would surely be a journey of the longest and bitterest sort, one lasting many lifetimes. But it must begin with a single step.

The question was, is this the first step forward?

The valley of Trama, mute and foreboding, might hold the answer.

Glamiss took the first crossing of the river for himself. That was like him, Emeric thought. If there were danger in that silent village, it was Glamiss who would face it first.

Blue Star picked her way daintily through the shallows, her slender legs flashing wetly in the sunlight. When she stood on the opposite bank near the mill, Glamiss signaled for the troopers to cross, two by two, with the remainder holding their lances and crossbows at the ready.

But the crossing was uneventful. The last to ford the river was Vulk Asa, leading the dead warman's mare and her mournful burden.

The scouts had crossed the river some half kilometer upstream and now they appeared, their mares' flanks glistening and still wet from the swim.

"Nothing in sight, Glamiss Warleader."

Emeric unconsciously raised his eyes to the glacier that seemed here to loom over the village. From his position near the mill he could not see the moraine and the high platform built into the mountain, but he was ever conscious of it. For it was there, he was certain, that the folk of Trama had taken refuge with their Warlock.

"They seem to have scattered most of the flocks," the second scout reported. "The hillsides were swarming with weyr.

Fat ones. But no people anywhere."

"We will scout the village," Glamiss said. He, too, knew where the folk had gone, Emeric realized. But he would not chance an assault on the mountain until he knew that the village was clear at his back. Emeric thought about Ulm and the entire levy of Vara landing behind them, pinning them all against the moraine with a volley of quarrels and throwing spears, and shuddered. A man in this time must always be prepared to die in battle, the Navigator thought, but it was a bitter thing to be caught and killed in so treacherous a little affair on this barbarous planet so far from Rhada—

"Stay with me, Emeric," Glamiss ordered, turning Blue Star toward the open space among the hovels that apparently served Trama for a marketplace.

From here one *could* see the platform high under the glacier. Metal glinted there, and that terrible, silvery clothing the Warlock wore. But Glamiss paid no heed. In the field, Emeric thought, his friend became a military machine: each tactical problem being attacked with precision in its proper place, until the strategic plan of whatever battle must be fought lay cleanly and clearly defined. Glamiss was a military genius and only his lowly estate prevented him from exercising his talents to the full. What would he be able to do with armies instead of warbands, with nations and planets instead of fiefs and barbarous berserkers to command?

The dream again, Emeric thought. It was only last night between the rising of the moons that Glamiss had told him of it. Yet here he was, as caught up in the strange wonder of it as Glamiss himself. Was this the force of the power men called destiny?

He shook his head exasperatedly. He had been in the hinterlands too long. Glamiss was only a lowborn mercenary leader of troops—not some great conqueror. He was a boy, really, barely even old enough to claim a man's state and weapons. Still—didn't every true conqueror begin this way? In Algol he had learned the legends of Philip of Macedon, of Temujin, whom men called Genghis Khan, of the man known as Bonaparte. All of these and others had begun as simple soldiers. The Navigator smiled thinly. If Glamiss should ever become what he imagined he might become he would have to prohibit the teaching of such legends lest other simple warmen dream of empires . . .

"What are you grinning about, Emeric?" Glamiss asked, as they moved between the buildings to the market square.

"Daydreaming, Glamiss," the priest replied.

"Save it for when we are safe within the mountain, my friend," Glamiss said.

"*In* the mountain, Glamiss Warleader?"

"Do you see anything *outside* the mountain worth taking?"

Suddenly, as if in answer to Glamiss's rhetorical query, the silence was torn by a screaming blast of sound: voices, brassy music, and the throb of great military drums. Glamiss wheeled Blue Star and signaled the troopers to take cover.

Emeric tried wildly to discover the source of the thundering noises, but there was nothing. Then his body felt a growing, icy chill of dread as he saw the swirling darkness forming in the marketplace. It was a blurry shadow that covered the width of the entire square, and it seemed alive with flashes of light that, curiously and terribly, seemed to be developing substance.

Glamiss sat astride the snarling Blue Star, his flail and sword drawn and ready. The warmen had melted into the alleys between the hovels, terrified (as was Emeric) but responsive to Glamiss's discipline.

When the Navigator looked again at the square, he was shocked to see that it was filled with warriors: strange men in armor not unlike his own iron mail, but decorated with brilliant tabards and surcoats bearing devices he had never before seen. The soldiers were gathered about a handsome young man with hair the color of gold, shimmering in the sunlight and blowing strangely to an unfelt wind.

Emeric looked about him desperately. Where had the soldiers come from? The square and the village had been deserted only an instant before and yet now the place swarmed with these brilliantly caparisoned and armed warriors. Glamiss signaled him to take cover with the others, but he himself sat astride Blue Star, watching the hundred or so soldiers in the square through narrowed eyes. He would have spoken to them, demanded to know whose men they were and what business they had in a village belonging to the lands of Lord Ulm

—but the words died in his throat, for the richly armed company was paying not the slightest attention to him, nor to the remainder of the troop—which they surely could not have avoided seeing.

"Emeric!" Falling back into the mouth of a narrow way leading into the square, Glamiss signaled to the Navigator.

"Holy Star protect us!" Emeric said fervently, making the same witchsign that had only a short while before so irritated him when made by the men.

"Emeric, *listen!*"

The sound of military trumpets and drums had faded and the words the strange warriors spoke came clearly across the square.

"What language is that?"

Emeric strained to make out the words. He had no trouble hearing, for the talk was now clearly audible, and the phrases and words perfectly pitched. But the language—Holy Star, it wasn't Empire Anglic—exactly. Yet it was so similar that it tantalized the listeners ear with familiar words and cadences.

"I don't know, it—"

"Listen!"

Emeric turned to stare. The fair-haired boy was addressing his soldiers. It was obvious that he was the greatest personage in that strange gathering, for when he spoke, all listened with respect.

—No, faith, my coz, with not a man from England: God's peace! I would not lose so great an honor, as one man more, methinks, would share from me, for the best hope I have. O, do not wish one more! Rather proclaim it, Westmoreland, through my host, that he which hath no stomach to this fight, let him depart; his passport shall be made, and crowns for convoy put into his purse: We would not die in that man's company that fears his fellowship to die with us—

Emeric studied the soldiers at the edge of the group. There was a strange and shadowy quality to them, as though one could almost see *through* their bodies. The Navigator shivered and made the sign of the Star. This was the Warlock's witch-work, and yet—and yet—those words the handsome boy war-leader was speaking. He *knew* those words, or some very like them.

"Glamiss—"

The Vykan gripped his mailed arm to silence him, listening. The boy now stood atop what appeared to be a magnificently decorated brass cannon. His voice had risen in pitch and timbre. The surcoat he wore glittered in the sunlight and his flaxen hair blew in that unfelt witch-wind.

> *This day is called the Feast of Crispian: he that out-lives this day, and comes safe home, will stand a tip-toe when this day is named, and rouse him at the name of Crispian. He that shall see this day, and live old age, will yearly on the vigil feast his neighbors, and say, "To-morrow is Saint Crispian:" Then he will strip his sleeve and show his scars and say, "These wounds I had on Crispin's day." Old men forget: yet all shall be forgot, but he'll remember with advantages, what feats he did that day!—*

The words and rhythms were becoming clearer in Emeric's mind. Anglic it was, yes, but not the language of the Empire. No, it was far older than that, it was the tongue called English, after the ancient island in the Atlantic Sea of mythic Earth. It was the way men spoke in that place in the beginning of history—in that legendary time called the Dawn Age!

> *—then shall our names, familiar in his mouth as household words, Harry the King, Bedford and Exeter, Warwick and Talbot, Salisbury and Gloucester, be in their flowing cups freshly remembered. This story shall the good man teach his son; and Crispin Crispian shall ne'er go by from this day to the ending of the world, but we in it shall be remembered; we few, we happy few, we band of brothers; for he that sheds his blood with me shall be my brother. Be he ne'er so vile, this day shall gentle his condition. And gentlemen in England now*

*abed shall think themselves accursed they were not here,
and hold their manhoods cheap whiles any speaks that
fought with us upon Saint Crispian's day.*

Emeric was startled to hear the sudden shout from Glamiss.
The Vykan dug his heels into Blue Star's flank and galloped
out into the marketplace toward the strangers. Emeric was
shocked to see that Glamiss was waving his weapons to assem-
ble the troop. And he was *laughing,* shouting with laughter,
making the square echo with it.

"Emeric!" the Vykan called. "Out! Come out here!"

The Navigator eased Sea Wind forward warily. Glamiss
turned to face him, his teeth showing white in an insane grin.
"It's a *play,* Emeric! They're *actors*!"

The realization was like a burst of light to the Navigator. He
remembered now the vague allusions to the image-projections,
the holographic films of the Empire. It was very like the
navigational holographs produced by the starships.

Then the significance of the images in the marketplace
began to broaden. So the Warlock had at his command the
magic (call it science, Emeric, he told himself) of the Empire
—some of it, at any rate. *Functioning* machines. The implications were staggering. Did Glamiss understand them as well?

The Navigator looked at his friend, who was galloping Blue
Star around the marketplace—passing *through* the projected
images with shouts of delighted laughter. The warleader was
behaving like a truant boy, swinging his flail through the holographs in glittering arcs while the fair-haired actor declaimed:
*"I pray thee, bear my former answer back . . . the man that
once did sell the lion's skin while the beast liv'd was killed with
hunting him—"*

The warmen of the troop moved cautiously into the square,
half-frightened and bemused by the sight of their leader
galloping through the seemingly-solid substance of the martial
host.

Glamiss stopped Blue Star in the center of the marketplace
and raised his eyes toward the looming glacier. "Warlock!
Warlock!" he roared, his voice tinged with wild delight. "I
know your secrets, Warlock! *I'm coming to take them!*"

There was not, Emeric realized, a chance that the silver-robed sorcerer on the mountain could hear Glamiss, and the Vykan knew it. But it was fitting to the marvelous insanity of the moment that Glamiss should shout a challenge like that. Emeric felt it and so did the others in the troop; the marketplace filled with their clamor. The men who were still apprehensive and wary of the shadowy warriors in the holofilm were sustained and buoyed up by their leader's defiance.

Glamiss, his head thrown back, weapons raised, was calling again to the owner of the mountain's magic. "I know you, Warlock! I know about dreams and illusions! You are my brother, Warlock! We're both mad and I'm coming for you now!"

The Navigator rode to Glamiss's side and spoke quietly. "Glamiss—"

The Vykan turned and said to Emeric, quite calmly, "Do you realize what this means, priest? Up there, somewhere on that mountain, there are *still machines with power to run them*—"

The Navigator made the sign of the Star. "Abominations, Glamiss. The Inquisiton was right. The Adversaries live in this cursed valley." His voice trembled with revulsion, remembering, as a priest should, the tales of the falling suns, the death of billions that accompanied the dissolution of the Empire.

"I want those machines, Emeric," Glamiss said in a dead level voice. His wild enthusiasm seemed muted now, and Emeric realized that it had been largely a show for the men, a display to hearten them for a foray up the moraine.

He frowned, thinking that his friend had been changing steadily ever since entering the valley of Trama-Vyka. Very gradually the simple warrior had been turning—into what? A schemer, a traitor to his bond-lord? Worse yet, into a blasphemer and a seeker after forbidden knowledge and power?

That was the worst of it—for Emeric, priest that he was and an officer of the Holy Inquisition, felt the same terrible temptations. If there were truly imperial machines in that place, what strange powers might they bestow on the man who took them for himself? The crown and feathered cape might not be a vain dream, after all. But at what price? Was he, Emeric Aulus Kevin Kiersson-Rhad, prince of the Northern Rhad, priest and pilot of the Holy Order of Navigators, failing in his holy mission as chaplain here? Were the Adversaries, Sin and Cyb, stealing the soul of his friend before his very eyes?

"If there are machines, Glamiss—"

"And there are," Glamiss interrupted him, pointing at the holographic figures his troopers were now tentatively examining.

"*If* there are—they are the business of the Order and the Inquisition."

Glamiss said evenly, "We spoke of this before, Emeric. I told you that what there is in this valley will be mine." His eyes were pale and cold as iron.

"Even at the risk of your soul?"

"At the risk of ten thousand souls. Ten *million*."

"Then may the Star show mercy," Emeric said in a heavy voice. And in his mind he saw the suns falling again and fleets of starships storming across the galaxy in war. Was it a vision? he wondered. Was God in the Star giving him some preview of the future?

Glamiss gripped his shoulder and spoke earnestly. "Don't judge me yet, old friend. Don't judge me at all, in fact. This may all be God's work." He smiled thinly. "Who really knows what waits for us up there on the mountain?"

Emeric, depressed, shook his head. "Not I, Glamiss."

"Nor I. All we know is what lies behind us. A sullen animal —my lord Ulm—and a thousand men to kill us. You heard the Vulk say it." He looked up at the glacier and the mountain with hungry eyes. "What would you have me do, Emeric? Shall we wait like weyr for the slaughter?" He favored the priest with his dazzling smile and Emeric could not suppress the lift it gave his heart. Glamiss had the gift of leadership, that was undeniable. It was his strength and his greatest danger. "Or shall we ride up the mountain like warriors and men to meet this warlock? Tell me what you will do, old friend."

Emeric of Rhada sighed and shook his head sadly. He looked up at the burning disk of Vyka in the sky—the personification of one of the many aspects of God. *"Salve me, Stella,"* he murmured. And to Glamiss he said, "There was never any real doubt what I would do for you, was there? I am too much your friend, Glamiss Warleader. It may be the damnation of our immortal souls.''

The iron-colored eyes grew dark and veiled. "And it might lead to Nyor, priest. We can only try." With that, he turned away and ordered the troop to form for the move up the moraine. And in the marketplace the images spoke on, unheeded. *"Now, soldiers, march away: and how thou pleasant, God, dispose the day!"*

Chapter Ten

If one were seeking a single word to express the spirit of the Interregnum, that word might well be *paradox*. Men lived the most barbaric lives while co-existing with the sophisticated remnants of First Empire civilization. For example: throughout the darkest period of that dark age, the Navigators owned a functioning computer on Algol II (though it might be more accurate to say that the computer owned the Navigators). The device was destroyed in the intra-clerical Stellar Heresy Rebellion during the reign of Torquas IV, but in the last years of the Interregnum, the machine was still being used to solve social problems in much the same way that it was used by the men of the Imperial Academy of Astrodemography a thousand years earlier. Similarly, the starships (in the control of the Navigators), perhaps the pinnacle of Imperial technology, carried near-barbarians not only from star system to star system, but from place to place on the surface of the various planets.

It has been suggested by no less an historian than Navigator Julianus Mullerium (Middle Second Stellar Empire period) that the emergence of Glamiss of Vyka as the dominant god-king figure of the late Interregnum, and his subsequent sweep across the galaxy at the head of the Vykan, Vegan, and Rhadan hosts, was due—at least in part—to his having, in some way, solved the basic paradoxes of the human socio- and astrodemography of that most critical moment in history.

> —Vikus Bel Cyb-1009, *Principles of Astrodemography, Cassette LXI,* Early Confederate period

—dielectric interphasers stabilize primary spatiotemporal valences, making access to the engine cores unnecessary—and extremely hazardous. Core servicing will be performed *only* by qualified personnel in Imperial Naval Starship Facilities (Class A7 or above). However, since the estimated service life of the stellar drive unit has been computed to be 10^6 Earth Standard Years, it is extremely unlikely—

—speed of star class vessels may be varied from 0 kps (hovering atmospheric flight) to 10^9 kps (intersystem transit). Crew training has been simplified to an extreme—

> —Golden Age fragments found at Station One, Aurora

Bishop-Navigator Kaifa sat alone in the great hall of the *Gloria,* his cowled head resting wearily against the intricately carved back of his episcopal throne. His eyes, deeply set in a harshly lined face, were closed and his gnarled right hand idly fondled the iron symbol of the Holy Star that hung from a chain about his neck.

Around him, in the ill-lit and flickering darkness of the hall, the air of the starship seemed to hum and quiver with the impulses that flowed in magical invisibility from the engine cores deep in the vessel's keel. The wall-torches were guttering low but the Navigator made no move to call an attendant to replace them. Outside the ship, he knew, there was sunlight—the yellow-green brilliance of the Vyka Sun—but the darkness of the great hall suited his mood and state of mind.

Though he could not hear them, the men of the Vara-Vykan levy filled two of the starship's lower bays—their horses and gear three more. The stink of unwashed bodies tainted the atmosphere and stirred the Bishop's memory. From the age of twelve he had periodically breathed the heavy air of starships filled with warriors. He had been but a boy when his father, the Lord-Amir of the South Hadj on Nasser, bonded him to the Order. For a moment the Bishop remembered the sandy wastes of his home planet—the tall date-palms rising starkly against the hot white sky. Nasser was a planet of the Procyon system—a wilderness of emptiness away from this part of the galaxy. Even Kaifa, high churchman that he was, and with thirty years experience as a Guide of Starships behind him, could not say with certainty *how* far away. Nasser's sky at night, he recalled with uncharacteristic nostalgia, blazed with the stars of the Inner Marches, for it lay near the center of the Great Sky. How long it had been since he had seen so glorious and friendly a sky at night! How bleak and empty seemed the skies of Aldrin (he used the ancient name out of ecclesiastical habit; the natives called the planet and the star both Vyka).

He rubbed at his eyes and returned to his scrutiny of the relic on the table before him. It was a star map, or rather a fragment of a map, printed on plastic more than two thousand standard years earlier. Since it depicted the stars, it was a holy object, and as such had been in the keeping of the Order of Navigators for many decades.

He pursed his thin lips. Like so much else that originated in the time before the Adversaries, Sin and Cyb, had brought down the Empire, it was enigmatic.

To begin with, it was a two-dimensional projection of three-dimensional space, so that only a vague approximation of the spatial relationships could be derived from it. Nor were distances indicated in any terms the Bishop could understand. It was, in fact, a page from a primer on astrography written for children of the Golden Age, to whom many far more sophisticated learning aids had been available. Still, it was a genuine relic, and the Navigator's fingertips caressed the smooth plastic lovingly and with reverence.

An incomplete sentence, in the spiky Anglic ideographs of the Empire, had been written across the bottom of the map. (By some long dead schoolchild? Kaifa wondered. "*The first cryonic storage facility in the Empire was built on Aldrin in 15—*" Strange are the ways of the Holy Star, the Bishop thought. Perhaps two thousand years ago a student had made a note on a map in a book to provide in this time the only certain confirmation of the Algol computer's warning of a coming social crisis.

Kaifa closed the illuminated cloth and leather binding that protected the relic lovingly. He rubbed his eyes again and estimated the time the *Gloria in Coelis* had been in slow-flight. No more than minutes to Trama now, he judged. It was almost time for him to go to the bridge.

He stretched his legs, wearied by the weight of his iron mail. I'm growing old, he thought, while still a young man. The demands of God in the Star were heavy.

He thought of his Order, a few thousand men spread across the vastness of the Great Sky. A few men, fewer starships. All working to keep alive the light of religion and knowledge . . . and for what? All Navigators, he thought, must have these doubts sometimes. There was so much to do and a man's life was so short. One could but spend oneself picking out, winnowing, and preserving the bits of wisdom that remained after the great and terrible fall of the Empire that ruled a thousand suns. And one could never be certain that what one did was truly holy, for Sin and Cyb were everywhere—waiting to strike the race down still again.

A man grew worldly in this mission, Kaifa thought. How much better, how much more holy, would the contemplative life be. But each man did what he was ordained to do. He, Kaifa, was a warrior at bottom and the councils of the Order were never mistaken in their assignment of tasks. Even the grim Talvas Hu Chien, the Grand Master whose Holy Inquisition had burned a million sorcerers and heretics, had been chosen for his work. He had not sought it any more than had Kaifa his own.

The gnawing question always was, however, how much of what a Navigator was ordained to do was truly the work of God—and how much was the work of the Adversaries? Even the computer on Algol was, after all, a machine—tainted with Sin. And in a more practical sense (for Kaifa was above all else a practical man) one had to wonder how effective the device really was. Great quantities of its memory had been excised and destroyed by zealots centuries ago. Other information had been fed into it: information that was questionable, to say the least. Irreplaceable components had been worn out and destroyed over the years by fanatics who demanded to know such things as "How many angels can stand on the point of a sword?" and "How many eyes has the Great Demon Cyb?"

At best, Kaifa thought, rising tiredly, it is doubtful that we priests have made the very best use of the few bits of science that survived the holocaust. But what was one to do? Man, after millennia in space, was still only Man, a weak and sinful—even foolish—vessel for life. Sometimes Kaifa secretly wondered if mankind was not some sort of dreadful joke foisted off on the Universe by an ironic God.

But, since he *was* practical, and since only the Order of Navigators maintained even a semblance of order among the worlds of the Great Sky, he accepted both Man and Universe as he found them. Civilization, he believed, was the business of Man. And bitter experience proved that it must, like Man himself, stand on *two* legs, not one. The Empire had been a single leg and it had stood perhaps three thousand years—an instant in universal time. In the so-called Golden Age there had been no church, no Order of Navigators, no real spiritual strength to form the second leg. And so the suns had fallen. Now, the Order existed—but there was no state, for the Empire lay in rubble. The problem, the task, seemed insoluble and endless. Perhaps Man really was a cosmic joke.

He frowned, fastened his homespun habit across his armored chest, made the sign of the Star, and started for the bridge, thinking of the science the Order would acquire in taking over the valley of Trama and wondering what, if anything, would be done with it.

*　　*　　*

Shana the Dark, standing on the platform above the moraine, her slender body pressed against the hard, familiar face of the mountain, had come to a conclusion. None of the other villagers whom the Warlock had impressed into service had yet reached the same conclusion because they were all terribly afraid of the "power" they imagined they had invoked.

But Shana was cleverer than the rest—cleverer than Shevil Lar, her father, even. Perhaps the same quality of mind that allowed her to touch the souls of the eagles gave her a clearer insight into the minds of men. She could not be certain of this, but she felt it deeply.

Her conclusion was simply this: the Warlock was crazy.

And out of this grew many other conclusions that bore strongly on the safety and situation of the folk of Trama.

For if the Warlock was crazy, it followed logically that he was not a great sorcerer (for sorcerers did not, in the very nature of their superiority to men, go insane). He was therefore a man. A very strange man, to be sure, and one possessed of a knowledge of many things that were strange to the inhabitants of Trama, but still a man with all the faults and weaknesses that condition entailed.

Shana wondered for a moment where such a man as the Warlock might really have come from—but being a practical woman as well as a clear thinker, she discarded this line of thought as unrewarding for the time being.

The folk had, with many misgivings, come into the mountain caves of the Warlock for safety. Those who had not, had by now scattered into the forests across the ridge-lines from the valley and might well never be seen again, for that was the way of life in these times.

But those of the folk who had taken refuge with the Warlock expected the old man to protect them from the soldiers Shana could now see forming up at the bottom of the moraine —the same soldiers who had so savagely defended themselves against her eagles earlier in the morning and who, worse yet, were accompanied by a priest of the Inquisition.

The magic the Warlock had invoked against the warmen had been showy and impressive. First, there had been the ghostly host that seemed to spring, somehow, from the devil-machines on the platform. After that had come the ranks of gray-uniformed men carrying swastika banners through the impalpable image-snow.

And now, even as she stood watching from behind the moaning, murmuring ranks of her fellow-villagers, mud-colored machines that resembled huge insects with white stars painted on their sides were crisscrossing the moraine in seemingly furious battle.

But the machines and the warriors were, every one, illusions. She saw that almost immediately. *And so had the soldiers of the lord Ulm.* They had realized with discouraging swiftness that they were opposed by nothing more substantial than shadows. Shana gave some thought to that and decided that their leader must be a brave man and a wise one—at least as wise as the Warlock, himself.

Later—if there *was* a later—she thought she would like to know how those boxes with the whirling prisms and shaped glasses formed the insubstantial but real-seeming images below. But she was reasonably certain that this was, in fact, the best the Warlock could do for the folk, and it was far from enough. If the people were to be saved from the warmen's depradations, they must take refuge inside the mountain again, and the Warlock must close the great metal doors. The thought of such confinement made her shudder, but it was the only hope unless some miracle happened.

One thing was certain. A crazy old man could perform *tricks,* but the sort of miracles required were very probably beyond his powers. She felt sorry for him and, to a lesser degree, for herself and her people.

She had tried very hard to make the eagles attack the soldiers again, but they had refused. The master-bird had been killed by a crossbow quarrel and the flock had become unruly. Grieving for the terrible execution among her falcons, she had nevertheless tried to bring them back to the attack. She had failed. Now, unless something happened very soon, the people of Trama would be at the mercy of Ulm's hardbitten warriors and, what was worse, at the mercy of the Inquisition.

That was why it seemed bitterly ironic to her that the mysterious silver-clad, blind magician to whom the villagers had prayed and sacrificed for three years—*They even wanted to sacrifice me,* she thought indignantly—was helpless against the armed and mounted men below. Helpless because he was simply a crazy old man.

She watched his back now as he capered and danced and shouted, his cracked old voice mingling with the sound of illusory explosions and mock battle in the lower reaches of the moraine.

"I'll teach you history, barbarians!" he was screeching, laughing wildly as the metal insects bathed the landscape in streams of dreamfire. *"Those are the American tanks at Kasserine! They fought there in the dawn of time, savages! Fear the past, animals!"*

But the soldiers he called barbarians, savages, and animals showed very little sign of falling into funk in the face of the ghostly war machines. Shana could see that they sat their mares without flinching, and when the tumult seemed about to weaken the resolve of one or another of their troop, the warleader—a handsomely made young man on a blue-skinned charger—rallied them to stand their ground.

In a matter of heartbeats, that proud young warrior would be totally convinced that this was the Warlock's worst. When that happened, he would order a charge up the moraine, and the villagers on the platform would be ridden down and killed if they resisted.

Impatiently, her fear for the folk crowding out her fear of the Warlock, Shana moved forward and tugged at the warm, shimmering mesh of the old man's gown. "Warlock! Warlock!"

Shevil Lar and that spineless creature Tamil Hind—who had once dreamed of marrying her, Shana thought angrily —turned to regard her, white-faced. The sight of her importuning the Warlock frightened them.

"Shana, no!" her father called fearfully. "He will strike you dead!"

But far from striking her dead, the Warlock seemed to be completely unaware of her or any of the folk who had foregathered here on the platform with the devil machines. The old man continued to shout and caper as though, Shana thought, the warmen in the moraine were completely subject to his will.

"Warlock, listen to me!" She clung to the slippery fabric of the robe, and a part of her mind learned what a fragile wisp of a body there was beneath the metal mesh. The thing on his shoulder hummed and clicked and whirred as he moved about. Nearby, it did not frighten the girl as it should have. Always before, when she had sat at the Warlock's feet learning to control the eagles, she had been too awed to study the device carefully. But now she realized that it was not, as some declared, the Warlock's familiar. It was, like the devices on the platform, simply some sort of machine.

"Warlock, hear me!"

The old man stopped capering and turned, his terrible blind eyes seemed to search for her. The glittering lens of the thing on his shoulder fixed on her at last and he spoke. "Ah, Shana? What is it? Can't you see I'm busy, girl?" His grin showed aged teeth. "I am giving the barbarians a history lesson, yes. You can see that, can't you? Now leave me alone, child."

"Warlock," the girl said urgently. "Sir. Lord. Please listen to me. The images are not frightening the warmen. See for yourself . . ." She waved her thin brown hands at the moraine desperately.

"I have all the soldiers of history to fight for us, girl," the old man said wildly. "They *must* be frightened!"

"No, Lord. See for yourself. Look at their warleader. The one on the blue horse. He's laughing at us, Lord. At *you*—please *look*—"

The Lord Ophir frowned at that and his temper surged. Barbarians laughing at a Rigellian prince? His memories tumbled, clotted, in his drug-damaged brain. *"I am the Imperial Heir! The King-Elector!"* he said in Anglic. The girl understood the language, but not the sense of what he was saying, he knew. Why didn't she understand him? She was a subject of the Rigellian Empire, as were those savage-looking horsemen at the foot of the hill. They were *all* dependents of the alt Messier family, all of them, and all that dwelt in this place, and all that lived on the planets of all the thousand suns!

God, he thought, why can't I remember properly? It was the

effect of trilaudid on the time-sense, the memory. Images came and went so swiftly—

"Warlock, Lord! We have to hide in the mountain," the girl was saying urgently. "You have to take us into your mountain and close the doors on them. Warlock, *listen*—" She seemed near to tears and Ophir was disturbed that the child should be so upset. What was it, he wondered, that was distressing her so? Wasn't she enjoying the holofilms?

The other villagers on the platform set up a clamor. "They're coming! They're attacking! Save us, Warlock!"

Ophir turned his prosthetic eye on the soldiers below. They were indeed moving up the slope, picking their way easily through the boulder-strewn moraine. The morning sunlight glinted on iron mail. The slotted eyes of the mares gleamed like turquoise.

Then, quite suddenly, the troop paused. Ophir saw the rider in homespun habit point skyward. Ophir looked and his old heart began to pound and lurch with mingled apprehension and a terrible joy. *A starship!* The immense tapered hull hung low over the ridges to the east, the drive fields shimmering and glowing opalescent on the metal skin.

As the Warlock watched the great vessel moved majestically up the valley between the towering cliffs. It filled the air with a humming organ-tone that rose and fell in concert with the brightening and dimming of the coruscating dimensional-displacement fields that surrounded it.

The sight of the starship broke through scarred synapses in the old prince's brain. This was not the *Delos,* he realized. It was a smaller, star-class military transport. In such ships had the legions of the Empire been carried across the galaxy to garrison duties, colonial wars, and ceremonial stations. The blazon of the Empire on the prow had been painted over, and symbols had been added: a stylized star, a crudely made spaceship, and the legend *Gloria in Coelis*.

As the hovering ship moved almost directly overhead, blotting out the sun-disk of Vyka with its great bulk, Ophir could see that the great machine was old, *old*. The hull, beneath the shimmering forces that dazzled the eye, was pitted with the debris of centuries in space. The glassy curve of the transparent bridge was scratched and dulled. Inside the bridge, even at this distance, one could see dark cowled figures moving.

The old man's heart almost broke then, for nothing that he had seen or experienced since his awakening from the Sleep had told him more clearly that his world was gone in the dust of time. He had a fleeting memory of himself, a young man, riding through the surf of the Rhadan Sea with Dihanna laughing at his side. Gone, all gone.

"Warlock, Lord." Shana stood by his side, looking up at the tears leaking from the blind eyes. The starship had frightened her even more than the near presence of the warmen in the moraine, for she could not imagine what the appearance of the holy machine might portend—nothing good, certainly. But at the same time, her young heart was touched by the old man's grief.

His thin, blue-veined hand caught at hers and held it. She did not move. The others were running precipitously into the tunnel, leaving the devil machines, shrieking that the Day of Wrath was upon them. Shana wanted to run, too, but she could not bring herself to break away from the grieving old man who stared blindly at the monster in the sky and wept.

Ophir felt his robe sensing his drug-need once again and preparing his maintenance dose. "No," he said brokenly. "Let me alone."

Shana, her hand still caught in his, and thinking he spoke to her, was confused. "What shall we do, Lord? Tell me."

"There is nothing to be done. Nothing."

Shana looked fearfully at the starship. The kilometer-long hull was rotating slowly, prow swinging toward the lower valley. Along the underside she could see sections sliding back, exposing dark caverns within.

The warmen in the moraine began to move again, at a gallop this time, streaming toward the opening in the mountain. Suddenly a rain of crudely shaped round stones began to fall from the open bays of the starship. They struck the ground with a thudding thunder, scattering the warband below. Mares screamed and soldiers shouted defiant curses. She watched the warleader astride his delicate blue mare. Behind him came the Navigator and a Vulk. Shana wanted to close her eyes and scream as she saw a boulder strike behind them, splinter into fragments, and crush several soldiers and their mounts.

Then the warleader was upon them, his mare leaping easily onto the platform. Shana felt herself being torn away from the Warlock, swept upward and across the young man's saddle. She fought to free herself, but as his mare sprang for the shelter of the tunnel something thundered across the concrete platform from above. It was a boulder dropped from the starship that broke into fragments as it struck the archway's metal frame.

Shana saw with sudden horror that the Warlock was down, bleeding and still as any mortal. She struggled to free herself from the warman's hold and failed. Then the mare galloped into the tunnel and the darkness. She fought again to be free and the warman, exasperated, struck her backhanded across the jaw, blotting out even the darkness.

Chapter Eleven

—therefore the tactics of defense during landing operations of capital ships is dependent upon the expected response from enemy high-energy weapons. With meson screens fully extended, the deployment of infantry is limited by the metric-ton capacity of the standard Mark XVII Matter Transceiver: that is to say, units of battalion strength and 18.6 seconds. Starships equipped with the newer Mark XX Transceiver may deploy units of regimental strength at interva—

> —Golden Age fragment found at Tel-Paris, Earth (believed to be part of an Imperial military field manual)

The tactic of bombardment from above with solid missiles, stones and fire-rains is suitable only to situations wherein the enemy has been discovered concentrated in the open. While it may be true, as legends state, that the falling suns were in ancient times carried in the keel-bays of starships, no real parallel can be drawn between a rain of stones and such mighty and sinful weapons. However, it is to be emphasized that the decision to bombard or not to bombard is the prerogative of the warleader, and *not* the Guide of Starships. The Guide, or Pilot, is a spiritual adviser only. It is the commander of the landing force who must make the tactical decisions, for good or ill.

—Prince Fernald proc Wye, *On Tactics,*
Early Second Stellar Empire period

Bishop-Navigator Kaifa, his face pressed to the transparent curving wall of the starship's bridge, loosed a string of most unclerical oaths as he watched the troopers below vanishing into the tunnel in the mountain. The three novice Navigators, chastened by his anger, stood at their consoles in attitudes of holiness and rectitude—the only attitudes they could assume now that they had followed, as was proper, the instructions received from Lord Ulm and his captains.

"Didn't *one* of you have the sense to tell those fools this could happen?" the Bishop demanded furiously.

"It was the warleader's choice, Reverend Father," Brother Anselm said fearfully. "So it is written in the Book of the Way."

The Bishop's eyes glittered dangerously under his red-fisted cowl. "Are you instructing me on the Way of the Navigator, Anselm?"

"No, First Pilot. Certainly not. Only—"

"Idiot," the Bishop hissed.

Brother Collis, the aristocrat from the Inner Planets, felt the urgings of honor, even though he disliked Anselm, and always would, for his holier-than-thou attitudes. "With respect, First Pilot, there was no way to know the rebels would take shelter *inside* the mountain."

Kaifa bit his lips. What Collis said was true. Of all aboard the *Gloria,* only Kaifa, himself, knew that the mountain was honeycombed with imperial building. And even he had tended to doubt it, since the information from the Algol computer was suspect. Still, only an ass like Ulm and a fool like Anselm could contrive to attack a mobile force of cavalry from above with stones while carrying a thousand troopers in the holds anxious for combat.

Ancient custom and privilege allowed this sort of stupidity.

The warmen, blind and ignorant in the holds, made the tactical decisions even though they were not permitted (under penalty of excommunication) to enter the consecrated ground of the bridge—the only place on board a starship commanding a view of the ground below.

It was true enough that the Navigator crew *could* influence these decisions indirectly, and so it was usually in war. This time, however, he, Kaifa, had allowed the novices to make the approach to the valley, and so it was, in the final analysis, his own fault. He should have flown the approach himself. He wondered what the Grand Master would have to say about his gross error in judgment. Nothing good, that was certain.

"Ground us in that meadow by the river," he said angrily, pointing at the terrain below. He gathered his robes about him and left the bridge without further comment. It would do no good to chastise the novices for having stuck strictly to the Book of the Way. But all hope for surprise was lost now in that foolish rain of boulders from the bombing-bays. Like it or not, Ulm would have to use his men in siege rather than in maneuver. The "rebels" and whatever else lay hidden in this cursed valley of Trama would now have to be taken the hard way. He would take a certain grim pleasure in explaining this to Ulm in the crudest, most insulting terms possible. Not the attitude of a charitable churchman, Kaifa thought grimly, but at the moment he felt neither charitable nor churchly. He would have to assign himself a suitable penance when all was over. Something severe, self-flagellation or a long fast at least. Ave Stellas and Salve Dominis would never expiate the sinful anger he felt at this moment.

The scene in the hospital tunnel was one of breathless confusion, but Glamiss moved with authority through the spaces crowded with men and horses, restoring order, counting casualties, letting himself be seen by troopers.

Emeric and the Vulk Asa had cleared a space where the light of the still open archway reached into the dimness, and there they ministered to the injured Warlock and the girl villager Glamiss had carried in, out of the rain of stones from the starship.

The villagers who had attended the devil machines on the

platform had vanished into the interior of the mountain, and so far no one had taken it upon himself to follow them. The warmen were grateful for the shelter of the tunnel, but they were badly shaken by the attack from the air and by their mysterious surroundings. The mares, most of whom had been moved away from the tunnel mouth, were growling and lamenting, upset by the unfamiliar footing and the dark cave in which they had suddenly found themselves.

The Navigator lifted the girl's head and bathed her forehead with a bit of cloth dampened from his waterbottle. Glamiss had probably not meant to injure her, but her cheek was bruised, and as she opened her eyes she grew plainly frightened. Little wonder, Emeric thought, with the featureless Vulk nearby and the confusion all around. The girl's eyes fixed on the Red Fist of the Inquisition decorating Emeric's cowl, and her breath seemed to catch. The Navigator muttered an oath and pushed back the cowl so that the symbol would be invisible.

"Better now?" he asked.

The girl nodded slowly.

Vulk Asa moved nearer. Emeric understood that he was using the Vulk mind-touch to sooth the peasant girl's fears.

She said tremulously, "The Warlock. Is he dead?"

"No," Emeric said. "Hurt, but not dead yet."

Tears glistened in the girl's eyes. "He's only an old man. A crazy old man. We thought he could save us."

Perhaps what she said was true, Emeric thought. It remained to be seen. To be safe, he made the sign of the Star on her narrow brow.

Shana tried to rise and managed to come to a sitting position. In spite of himself, Emeric recoiled a bit from the smell of the poorly cured weyr skins she wore. It was difficult to think of people so poor as enemies of the Order and subjects for the interrogations of the Holy Inquisition. There was something terribly wrong with the social order that brought the folk of the Great Sky only fear and death.

The girl sensed his revulsion and a look of bitter pride touched her unformed features. She moved away from the priest, pressing her slender shoulders against the curving rock wall of the tunnel. Emeric had a flashing insight. This must be the adept; she seemed almost as skilled as the Vulk in reading those about her.

"Where is my father, Nav?" she asked. "What have you done to the others?"

"Was your father one of those at the devil machines?"

The term "devil machines" made Shana remember the Inquisition again and she said, "They were the old man's magic, Nav. The Adversaries had nothing to do with them."

Emeric could not help but smile at her courage. "Are you so certain of that—?" He paused, waiting for her to identify herself.

"I am Shana the Dark, daughter of Shevil Lar, the hetman, and Shevaughn Six-fingers," she said proudly, half-defiantly.

Six-fingers, Emeric thought. That would account for her mind-talent. Her mother was a mutation, Star-touched.

Asa laid his long hands on the girl's head and leaned toward her in the darkness. She shivered, but did not flinch. Another evidence of courage, Emeric thought. These people feared the Vulk and believed the Protocols.

"All is well, Shana," the Vulk said quietly.

Shana looked about her at the seeming turmoil: warmen taking up defensive positions at the tunnel mouth, the warleader calling orders, the mares snarling and calling to their masters. "It does not seem so to me, Vulk," she said tartly.

Emeric said, "A little respect, daughter. This is Vulk Asa—" He started to say, the Talker of the Lord Ulm and then realized that neither the Vulk nor any member of the troop could now expect anything but a sword blow from the Lord of Vara-Vyka. "This is the Talker of the Warleader Glamiss," he said.

"The one who struck me?"

"The same."

"Ulm's men are in the starship?"

"Yes."

"Then you are rebels?"

"Not by our choice, but it seems Ulm thinks us so."

Her expression relaxed slightly. "Then there will be no Inquisition here? No burnings?"

Emeric tightened his lips and made a decision that would

change his life. He made it with a single word. It was as simple as that. "No," he said.

The Warlock stirred and moaned. Dried blood clotted his thin gray hair. Shana went to him and held out her hand for Emeric's dampened cloth. The Navigator gave it to her and she began gently to bathe the old man's face. Emeric was struck by her gentleness: an unusual characteristic among the commonality in these bitter times.

"You didn't tell me about my father," the girl said. "Is he alive?"

"Unless there are dragons within these caves, he is," Emeric said. "None of the men at the machines were struck by the stones, but they have all scattered in the mountain."

The girl regarded him evenly. "Most of the folk are here. We were afraid of you, Nav."

"Because you withheld tribute from Ulm?" he asked. But he knew better. It was the hated Red Fist that had alarmed the weyrherders of Trama.

"Dihanna—"

Navigator and weyrgirl turned to look at the Warlock. The old man was breathing stertorously and Emeric sensed that he was badly injured. The deforming metal growth on his shoulder was dented and cracked by the force of the stone fragment's blow.

"Warlock. Lord. You have been injured. Do not try to speak," the girl said.

"Dihanna, where are we? I am blind, Dihanna," the old man said. A crooked smile touched his lips and he said, quite rationally, "I am a prince of the House of Rigell, I am the Lord of Rhada and the King-Elector—and I cannot *see*. What use is a blind Heir, Dihanna?"

Emeric stared at the old man. A prince of the Rigellian House? Impossible. The last Rigellian Galacton died in the sack of Nyor more than a thousand years before. *And Lord of Rhada? My homeworld*, Emeric thought. *What had this ancient witchman to do with Rhada?* He glanced at Asa, and the Vulk nodded. "He believes himself to be all those things, Nav Emeric."

"He's crazy," Shana said patiently. "The folk think him a

mighty warlock, but he's just a poor, crazy old man.''

Vulk Asa said softly, "The hereditary holding of the Heir to the throne of the Rigellian Galactons was Rhada, Nav Emeric. And the man was always known as the King-Elector."

Emeric exclaimed, "Are you telling me this warlock is a thousand years old, Vulk? Have you lost your reason?"

"I do not say. I do not explain. I simply tell you what is so," Vulk Asa murmured.

The Navigator stared at the Vulk. Damn them for unreadable aliens, he thought in a sudden rush of xenophobic anger. What, in the last analysis, did anyone know about the *Vulk*? Some said they were immortal—a patent absurdity. Still, they seemed to live on and on and on. They could be *killed* easily enough, but had anyone ever seen one die naturally? Never. They had apparently never built machines, yet in the early Dawn Age, Vulk had been discovered on the worlds of Beta Crucis and told a tale of the destruction of their own home-world of Vulka aeons before. Yet how did they reach the Crucian planets? The Protocols claimed that they had once had the power to travel across the Great Sky driven by the force of their own Vulkish thoughts and that God in the Star had punished them by taking this gift of the Adversaries from them. It was a thing beyond Emeric's understanding, but one thing was certain: the Vulk knew things men did not and no amount of torture or persecution had ever torn their dark secrets from them. So if Vulk Asa said that the Rigellian Heir had once held Rhada and was known as King-Elector—it was *so*.

Emeric studied the injured old Warlock with growing mystification and dread. Was this a man of the Golden Age miraculously preserved beyond his normal span of perhaps a hundred standard years?

He thought of Glamiss's dream of the feathered cape and star-crown and shivered with the awareness of fate's strange workings.

Chapter Twelve

This, then, is how it was, and how it shall be:
The people were dissatisfied and complained,
And Sin and Cyb said to the people: Act, you have
Nothing to lose but your chains!
But the Adversaries are deceivers, and therefore
The suns fell.
Weep, Man for you have learned nothing.
> —From *The Book of Warls,*
> Interregnal period

Then following wars such as had never before occurred in our galaxy. Fleets of worlds, natural and artificial, maneuvered among the stars to outwit one another, and destroyed one another with jets of sub-atomic energy. As the tides of battle swept hither and thither through space, whole planetary systems were annihilated.
> —Account of a vision attributed to one
> Olaf Stapledon, a Prophet of the Dawn
> Age

"What is history, Teacher?"

"It is the patina of small events on the surface of the Universe."

—Emeric of Rhada, Grand Master of Navigators, Early Second Stellar Empire period

Most men, Emeric knew, tended to fear the unknown and their fear made them ineffective. It was Glamiss's genius that he could organize and function with half the facts needed by ordinary men.

This was what was happening now, in the confusion of the sheltering tunnel. Vulk Asa had warned Glamiss of Ulm's intentions, but the attack from the air had been unexpected. Similarly, the Warlock's tactic of trying to frighten the troop away with the images in the village square and in the lower moraine implied a vast technology that Glamiss simply had no capacity to understand. Nor did he know what lay within the mountain. But he had, nevertheless, remained steadfast in his determination to take Trama and whatever it contained for himself. He had probably, Emeric conceded, been almost as frightened by events as any of the members of the punitive force, but his mind and spirit had remained purposeful.

Now he had stationed men to give the tunnel mouth a protection in depth, had sent others within the honeycomb to explore and locate the folk of Trama. He had sent the horses into a large reception area located by scouts at the end of the entrance tunnel and had divided the forty-five men remaining to him into siege-watches. A single pair of troopers had been stationed outside, near the stone-smashed wreckage of the devil-machines, to watch for the approach of Ulm's levy.

Ulm had been a fool to rain stones on the troop, Glamiss thought as he made his way through the crowded corridor. Unless there were many other entrances to this watch-warren in the mountain, a single section of warmen could hold the tunnel mouth indefinitely against him. But there were questions of supply to be settled—the troop would need food and water, the horses had been recently fed but would eventually need fresh meat.

Nothing was really resolved yet. This place—he looked

about him at the smoothly finished walls and the inoperative lighting globes in the overhead—reminded him very strongly of the interior of a starship. And like a starship, it seemed to be partially in operation. Also like a starship, it was incredibly *old*. A thousand questions clamored for answers, yet somehow he felt certain that this hollow mountain was the most valuable and the most important place on the entire planet—possibly in all the Great Sky. For here, in some peculiar way, the Empire still lived: feebly, perhaps, but miraculously.

He located Emeric and the Traman girl he had dragged into the mountain across Blue Star's withers. They were with Asa, crouching over the silver-clad Warlock. The old man was badly injured and probably would not survive. Glamiss's warrior's instinct told him that immediately. He was not sorry for the old fellow as a man—wasn't he a Warlock, and therefore suspect? But the secrets of this strange, ancient place must be locked up inside that grizzled head. For the moment the situation was stalemated, but any victory even over the Vara-Vykan levy now disgorging from the starship in the valley depended on the powerful mysteries of this place.

"Can he speak?" Glamiss asked.

"He's raving mad," Emeric said.

The old man gave a cracked laugh and said in a very rational tone, "The gift of trilaudid is a few hours of sanity before one dies. What a pity it can't give me back my eyes."

Glamiss raised his eyebrows at Emeric. "What is that supposed to mean? And what dialect is that?"

"I don't know what it means," The Navigator said. "The language is Imperial High Anglic."

In any other place Glamiss would have been surprised by the use of the old tongue, a language that all but priests understood imperfectly. But here it seemed quite natural. "What is 'trilaudid?'"

The Navigator shrugged helplessly, but the old man replied in a voice whose arrogance was not diminished by its weakness. "Who is that speaking? It sounds like a soldier, God help us. Wouldn't you know there would still be soldiers." He drew several shuddering breaths. "Trilaudid was a vision of paradise in my time, warrior. We used it to escape from people like you."

The girl now spoke to Glamiss for the first time. She had been staring up at him and he seemed like a sun god to her, gray-eyed, caped and armed. But she remembered he had struck her, and she had a touch of falconer's pride. "He's sick and old," she said. "And he's hurt. Don't trouble him now."

Glamiss regarded her with wry amusement. "You're braver than your folk, girl."

"My name is Shana. I am the hetman's daughter," she said, standing. Would he strike her again, she wondered, and braced herself for the blow. Warmen were like that, her father had told her, remembering his experiences among Lord Ulm's men.

"Very well, hetman's daughter. Suppose you come with me and find the rest of your people. I need them."

Her eyes flashed defiantly. "For the Inquisition?"

"I'm no Navigator," Glamiss said shortly. "I need them because we will be under siege here almost immediately. I intend to defend this place and your people will have to help me."

"Against Lord Ulm?" The girl sounded incredulous. "Are you rebels, then?"

"You saw the starship attack us," Glamiss said impatiently.

"You promise no harm to the folk?"

Glamiss caught her shoulder in a strong hand and squeezed it painfully. "Don't bargain with me, Shana-the-hetman's-daughter. Your people will take their chances, just as my men must. Be satisfied with that or I'll hunt them down like rabbits."

The Warlock's voice came raspingly, and he did not sound at all mad. "Listen to the soldier, Shana. Believe what he tells you when he talks of hunting people down. *That* you can always believe. Soldiers speak the truth when they speak of violence." Then he moaned and seemed to be taken by a spasm of delirium. "The soldiers always had the answers, didn't they, Dihanna? Purification by the fire cures everything—" He began to laugh and gasp and finally subsided into deep-breathing near-silence.

Glamiss ignored the Warlock. To Shana he said, "Do you know this place well?"

"Not well. I used to come here, but—"

"You came here alone? To him?" Glamiss indicated the old man.

"It's not what you think," Shana said angrily. "I came to learn the eagle-tongue. He has machines that teach here—"

Glamiss's eyes darkened with anger. "*You* are the one who sent the birds against us?"

Shana swallowed hard to suppress her sudden fear. He looked capable of killing her right now. "Yes," she said. "I defended the valley—my folk—"

"You killed one of my men. You wounded my mare."

"You were coming to burn us! To steal our weyr for Lord Ulm!" the girl protested.

"Enough! God's peace!" Emeric cried out, standing between them. "What's done is done, in the Star's Name! Let it rest. We have other things to think of now. This man needs help—"

Glamiss was about to reply when a voice, mellifluous to the point of being unctuous, sounded through the crowded corridor. It was the voice of the hospital computer and it came through an overhead speaker grill.

The computer's programming was idiotically unsuited to the present situation, but with cybernetic innocence, the device did its proper best.

"There are unregistered guests in the north entryport. Would all visitors kindly report to Hospital Administration on the fourth level for proper identification and decontamination, if you please."

The warmen stared upward in shocked disbelief at the witch voice, trying to locate its source.

The computer declared: "There are a number of animals in Reception Three. This is strictly forbidden by hospital regulations."

"It is the voice of the mountain," Shana whispered nervously, drawing nearer to Glamiss. "I've heard it before."

The computer continued primly: "Lord Ophir, if you please, return to your room at once. Your envirobe is inoperative and it is time for your medication. Lord Ophir, if you please, return to your quarters at once. It is time for your nutrient bath—"

The voice stopped abruptly with a sound of shattering com-

ponents as a warman, more nervous and perhaps more percep-
tive than his fellows, discovered the speaker grille and pierced
it with a thrown lance.

The Warlock drew a deep throaty breath and essayed another of his broken laughs. "Who was it shut up that moronic
machine? Did someone cut its transistorized throat? Bring him
to me and I'll reward him! A million hectares of Rhada to that
man, whoever he is!"

Glamiss was studying the shattered speaker grille with
dawning understanding. "It's something like the images in
the village, Emeric. A record is made somewhere and the
machines reproduce it. But"— he frowned, his Dark-Age
mind struggling with ancient, legendary concepts —"the
images spoke blindly, by rote. The voice of this place knows
we are here. Explain it to me, Nav."

Emeric, whose knowledge of computers was limited to the
very secret hint of instruction he had received as a novice con-
cerning the Algol device, was unable and unwilling to essay
more than the single comment that the ways of God in the Star
were not for men's understanding.

This brought still another cackle of glee from the old
Warlock. "That sounds like the voice of the clergy," he
wheezed. "The church instructing the military—the halt leading the blind! Things have not changed so much as all that,
after all! Uncle!" he called. "Can you hear them? Wherever
you are, *if* you still are, in heaven or in hell, do you hear them?
The church and the army are sharing their ignorance with one
another again! Now do you still blame me for finding my own
way? Were my drugs and dreams so terrible?"

"He raves, Nav Emeric," Shana said. "Can't we help
him?"

Emeric looked at Glamiss. The warleader said, "Come with
me, daughter of the hetman. Let's see what this place can offer him."

"You are taking my eyes!" screamed the Warlock. "Shana!
My prosthesis is broken! Tell the computer, Shana! *Tell it at
once!*"

Emeric noted that the Warlock had spoken harshly of the
computer, but he now demanded that it—somehow, miraculously—do something about his blindness.

Somehow, the Navigator thought wryly, one felt that this old creature was, or had been, a personage of great consequence: privileged, protected, and indulged. Like all who were so protected and indulged, he despised the source of his privileges. Yet as reality infiltrated the sick old mind, it screamed for still more privilege and protection, and from the very source so recently cursed and reviled.

The Warlock might be a man of the golden Age. In an infinite Universe anything was possible. But he was very, very like the men known to Emeric of Rhada.

That realization comforted the Navigator as Glamiss led Shana away into the catacombs within the magic mountain.

He did not notice the knowing and gentle smile on the face of Vulk Asa, who had listened and remembered and who now understood what this place was and the true identity of the Warlock of Rhada.

The legends and the Protocols said that the despised Vulk had a lifespan of twenty thousand years—and the legends and the Protocols were right.

For the Vulk was a truly ancient race, starvoyagers while men's ancestors, the australopithecines, were discovering the art of murder.

The Vulk themselves had their legends, which were not as the legends of men. According to their Triad dreams (their linking of racial memory chains in units of three), their ancestors had come across a hyperspatial void when Earth was still a molten ball, thrust through a fold in the cosmos by the power of their minds: a trillion living Triads giving psychokinetic energy enough to move a planet out of a universe threatened with some nameless destruction.

In those times the Vulk were a mighty people, capable of teleporting themselves throughout the known galaxy. But time and entropy were the enemies of all living things, even the Vulk. And so it was that long before men discovered them (first on the worlds of Beta Crucis and later elsewhere), they grew enfeebled and had lost the power to roam at will through near space.

The Vulk were *old*; Man was young. The Vulk were timid, with the fragility of age; Man was aggressive, with the brute strength of youth. Yet in Man they saw themselves—as they had been in another cosmos before time began in this alien universe. And with great wisdom they understood that what Man would become in the next million—the next ten million—years, was yet to be decided. To the last scattered remnants of the once mighty race of Vulka, Man was an opportunity to survive, to achieve. He was vitality, hope for a future—and always a danger to himself and his galaxy. They did not read the future, for they understood that the future is many possible things and events. But they sensed the *possibilities* of the future, and this was the tie that bound them to Man.

They had seen his first Stellar Empire come into being: massive, materialistic, robust, brutal. They had seen it fall, riven by racism, political dissent, burdened with a plethora of *things*.

Many Vulk now living had seen this fall of night with their own inner eyes. There was a Vulk on Rhada, Gret by name, who had walked the soil of Earth in Shakespeare's time. Another, in Algol now, had felt the heat of Man's first nuclear blast, hidden in the desert rocks at Alamogordo. Vulk Asa, himself, had been born on a world of the star Sirius during the time men called the Golden Age. He had lived nearly seven thousand standard years and was young, as the Vulk reckoned age.

The millennia, the wanderings, the pogroms had winnowed out the weak and foolish among the aliens. The Vulkish people had grown very wise. And not the least of their wisdom was their understanding of the younger, more savage race with whom they shared this galaxy. Their rule was this: watch, learn, help when you can. *But do not presume to guide. Do not interfere.* Man's destiny was his own—even though it now was the destiny of the ancient race as well. The young, they knew, must shape their own world. Man had once spread himself to the stars and had nearly destroyed himself. Now he was stirring once again for another effort at Community. The Vulk understood that it would come—or not. Though their own existence depended on the still half-animal race that barely tolerated them, they dared help in only the smallest, most gentle ways. For if men should come to know *all* about the Vulk, they would turn on them in genocidal fury. That,

Vulk Asa and all his people knew, was the present nature of Man.

And so Vulk Asa, resting quietly within the dark corridor of an Imperial Cryonics Hospital, surrounded by savage, ignorant warriors, touched minds gently with his sister-wife Rahel—who would live indefinitely unless some political overthrow changed the ways of Vara-Vyka, in the stone keep of a barbarian warlord.

I long for the sunlight, Asa, and the starry night.

Patience, Sister. It will come.

I am half-blind without a Third for Triad, Brother. Are you stronger? Can you look ahead?

A little way, Rahel. And the signs are good. Dangerous and strange, but good. Glamiss grows in heart and mind.

He is young—even for a man. Very young.

The young will lead the young, Rahel. The knowledge he needs is here, though he does not know it. He hopes for things—for weapons. But perhaps—

Will we ever be free, Asa?

Believe it, beloved.

In their intimacy, their thoughts became stranger, more alien, beyond the understanding of any man. And they contained a thin bright thread of hope. The only two Vulk on the planet discussed Glamiss no more, but both began to hope that he might be the one to strike the spark that would, in the far future, flare into a light of civilization once again—for both Vulk and Man.

Chapter Thirteen

It is my hope, Majesty, that it will soon be possible to "record" personality and impress undifferentiated protein molecules with the patterns I have recorded. Should this be, as I have reason to believe, possible, the medical and sociological ramifications will be immense for our people. The learning of great men need not be lost to clinical death. The teaching process may be made infinitely more efficient. And even the notion of cyborg replicas of human beings is not too outré to be considered.

For these reasons, and for others too technical to present to you in this form, I beg Your Majesty to continue your most gracious support of the research being conducted by the Committee on Personality Transfer of the Imperial Medical Services Authority.

> —Fragment of a petition requesting the
> continuation of an Imperial Research
> Grant. From the Imperial Archives
> of Nyor, Golden Age period

In that place in the mountain, beneath the glacier called Trama, the minds of men were stolen from them and sometimes placed in iron boxes. If this were all, it would be bad enough. But there is no limit to the wickedness of the Adversaries. They sometimes released these captive minds in the heads of golem, which we call Cyb, and (may the Star punish them!) even in the minds of other men.

—From the Interregnal legends of Vyka

Glamiss and the girl, Shana, discovered the folk cowering in the shadowy cavern that once had been the exercise area of the ancient hospital. Glamiss's quick mind divined the purpose of the great hall almost immediately, for though many of the therapy machines were incomprehensible to him, much of the old games equipment was still intact, still racked up along the featureless walls.

The lighting was poor, for only a half dozen of the scores of glow-globes in the distant overhead still functioned. The effect was to cast long shadows and increase the sense of open space. The hall was very large. It was, perhaps, the largest single room Glamiss had ever seen: far bigger than the keep of Ulm's donjon by the sea. The ceiling could not have been reached by fifty men standing on one another's shoulders, and the free-form floor was a full three hundred meters across its narrowest part.

The place held all the folk of Trama easily. They huddled in the shadows at the rounded end of the great room, and as Glamiss and the girl appeared from a corridor, a moan of despair rose from the villagers.

Glamiss marched across the wide floor and faced them, his hands on his hips, face stern under his helmet. "I have not come to harm you," he said harshly.

A stocky man in weyr skins, one of those who had been on the platform with the devil-machines, Glamiss noted, came reluctantly forward.

Shana pushed past the warleader and ran to the Traman. "Shevil," she said, "tell the folk not to fear."

The villagers muttered among themselves, and Glamiss impatiently heard the word "Inquisition" again and again. He raised his weaponless hands to show them his intent.

"You do not need to fear the Inquisition," he said. "There will be no burnings in Trama."

The hetman Shevil inched forward, his head dipping with a villager's sullen courtesy. "There is a Navigator with you, Lord. The people do not believe there will be no burnings."

Glamiss's eyes glittered contemptuously. "Are you so wicked as all that, then?"

Shana turned on him angrily, "Do not use that tone to my father. He is hetman here."

Glamiss inclined his head with mock politeness. These people were peasants, weyrherders, the nearest thing to animals in all the Great Sky. He could not regard them as anything else. Yet the girl-adept had courage. As a warman, he could at least accept that. And if these creatures were to be useless, at least they must not be a hindrance when Ulm's levy tried to force the tunnel mouth as they surely would—and soon.

"Hetman of Trama," he said formally, "I say there will be no burnings. The Nav is my close friend. He does not really believe in burning sinners anyway—"

"He wears the Fist," one of the villagers said fearfully, and the others took up the complaint. "The Fist. The Red Fist of the Inquisition."

"Not by his choice, good people," Glamiss said. And he thought, *good people, indeed—I sound like a politician.* "I am Glamiss Warleader—and it's true I came into this valley to take your weyr to Ulm. You could have spared yourself this by obeying the laws, you know. No one would ever have known about your Warlock or this place if you had sent your tribute as custom commands—"

"We were hungry, Warleader. Ulm is—"

Glamiss interrupted the hetman sharply. "I know what Ulm is. Better than you. You saw him attack me, man. You saw him drop the stones from the starship. *I break my pledge to Ulm. I break it now.*"

The villagers murmured and Glamiss pretended not to hear the fear-tinged voices that said: *"Oathbreaker."*

A heavy business, the abandonment of serious oaths. The villagers knew it and Glamiss knew it even better than they. And, he wondered, how thin have I worn my honor by this? It was true that Ulm had attacked—but hadn't he, Glamiss, decided to break his pledge to the Lord of Vara-Vyka *before* the attack? Last night? Or, in the Star's truth, long, long ago?

Glamiss put aside these dark thoughts and spoke again. "Ulm is in the valley now—savaging your houses most probably, though you don't have anything worth stealing. But he'll tire of that soon and come up here to the mountain for me—for *you*, for all of us."

A younger Traman dared to speak up. He said bitterly, "You have killed us, then. There are Navigators in the starship—maybe hundreds of them . . ."

"No more than three—possibly four," Glamiss said dryly. "And if they never get into this place, what will they know of your witch worship? Nothing at all." He hurried on before they could find fault with that statement, or remember the presence in the mountain of Nav Emeric. "I can keep them out. With my troop I can keep them out of this place until Vyka freezes. But we will need food and water and fare for the horses if we are to withstand a siege. You must provide them." He fixed them with a cold and appraising stare. "Is there another entrance to these caves?"

"If there is, we do not know of it, Warleader," the hetman said hopelessly.

"Is there food and drink here, then? The old Warlock doesn't look starved."

"He eats magical foods, Warleader," Shana said. "Pills and worms from tubes. We could not eat such things, nor could you or your mares."

"Then there's nothing for it but a foraging party," Glamiss said bluntly. "You, hetman. What's your name again?"

"Shevil Lar is his name, Leader of Brigands," Shana said angrily. "Shevil Lar, Hetman of Trama."

Glamiss suppressed an impulse to grin at her anger. "I think the wrong person is hetman of Trama," he said. "But never mind. Shevil Lar, then. You must make up a foraging party to go out and drive in some weyr and bring water from the river. Ulm's men will still be in the village looting for a time. If you hurry, you might make it before he scrapes a siege plan from the empty bowl of his head."

"But, lord—we are ony herdsmen—we—"

Glamiss silenced him with a gesture of angry contempt. "Don't tell me what you are. I know what you are. I am offering you a chance to be men." He looked down at Shana's thin, dark, and intense face. "Organize this, witch woman. Do it now. I'll see to it that a party of a dozen men is let through the tunnel to the outside. But you had better hurry. Even Ulm won't keep rooting around in your weyr-sty forever. There is a Bishop-Nav with him and *he* will want to break in here at any cost. Move now, girl."

"Yes. At *once*, oh, leader of bandits and robbers," Shana said tartly.

"Use your eagles to scout Ulm's movements," Glamiss said.

"*I* know what to do, *Lord*," the girl said and went to her father.

Glamiss considered saying something more to the huddling villagers; perhaps mapping out a plan for them, or even arming them. But he decided against it. They were herdsmen, as Shevil Lar said, and they knew how to catch their own weyr. They were *not* warriors and he hadn't time or the inclination to make them into fighting men. All that could come later—if they survived the next days. Meanwhile, he must work with Emeric, who was the only learned man among them all, to unravel some of the mysteries of this imperial place. On that, their ultimate survival might presently depend.

Without further comment, he turned on his heel and went back the way he had come, leaving Shana to deal with the panicky folk of Trama to whom he had bound, all quite inadvertently, his own destiny.

He found the Navigator in a long room at the end of a branching corridor. It was a room such as Glamiss and, he was sure, Emeric had never before seen.

All the lights functioned properly here, so that the place was brightly lit. And never had Glamiss seen such strange and gloriously decorated luxury. Walls and partitions had been painted with strange pictures that were curiously three-dimensional. The scenes depicted were of richly garbed people in gardens, working at incomprehensible tasks with strange yet graceful machines, of starships under construction, of a dozen or more activities he could not guess at. Imperial light-paintings these were. Glamiss had heard of such art treasures, but not one man in a hundred thousand on the Rimworlds had ever actually seen any.

Many of the paintings along the fifty-meter walls were of strange abstractions: patterns of light and color that seemed to suggest the shape of many things and yet could not be pinned down to represent anything familiar. Like many a barbarian before him, Glamiss felt curiously unsettled by these works. They created a disturbing craving for a sophistication he did not possess and he looked away from them to the end of the gallery, where Emeric sat gingerly on the edge of a chair—one of a half dozen forming a semicircle within a translucent shell shaped like half of a huge egg.

The Navigator was studying a narrow panel of toggles and broad, shallow buttons that glowed like jewels, lit from within by some mysterious source. As Glamiss approached him, he looked up, his face alight with excitement.

"Come look, Glamiss Warleader! I'll show you wonders!"

Glamiss touched the smooth, milky substance of the half-egg curiously. Though he had seen very few artifacts made of plastics, he knew in a general way, what the material was. The men of the Empire had made use of it in many ways, and since it was almost indestructible, it had survived the Dark Age in many places. But here it was perfectly preserved, unstained and unmarked. Glamiss wondered how strong it really was. He was tempted to try his sword against it.

Emeric, he could see, was filled with a barely controlled enthusiasm for whatever it was he had found. There were times, Glamiss thought, when he envied the priest his ecclesiastical education. Whatever there was of science (forbidden word!) remaining in the Great Sky was centered in the teaching universities of the Navigators in the Algol system. But it was not Glamiss's nature to allow another's enthusiasm to control his own. "Peace, Nav," he said. "First things first. Where is the Warlock?"

Emeric made an impatient gesture. "Asa found his rooms and has taken him there. At first the troopers balked at carrying the old man, but you know how Asa can persuade."

"Better than most," Glamiss said thoughtfully.

"Now, please, look at this. Have you ever seen anything like it?"

Glamiss stepped into the shelter of the half-egg and sat down in one of the chairs beside the Navigator. The contours seemed to enfold him, accommodating themselves to his body. It startled him, but his face remained impassive. He removed his helmet and ran a hand over his rumpled hair. He felt suddenly very tired. He thought of the forces gathered outside the mountain against him. A thousand men or more. A starship. Priests who outranked his own young chaplain. And somehow he felt that he was being maneuvered, *manipulated*. He knew that the idea of revolt against his bond-lord Ulm had been in his mind for a long while. But was *this* the proper time to move? He didn't know—he could not even be certain that the choice had been made in his own mind. It could have been made for him. He could be, he thought, as much captive of unknown forces as those shadowy warriors they had encountered in the marketplace of Trama—

"—that I should actually see something like this!" Emeric was saying excitedly. "I never would have believed it."

"What is it?" Glamiss asked wearily. "What is this thing?"

"You haven't been listening," the Navigator said reproachfully.

"I'm sorry. Tell me about your wonders."

"It's a *computer* terminal. At least, I *think* it is. It's not exactly like the—" He broke off, reluctant to speak of the machine in Algol. But, then, he thought, I am already damned if what I have agreed to do is displeasing to the Star. He said, "There is a device similar to this one in Algol. The Order uses it as—well, as an oracle of sorts. It answers questions, solves problems."

Glamiss felt a stirring of interest. He knew that he should move along, inspect the guard at the tunnel mouth, see the foraging party of villagers off. There were many things that needed doing, but this room and what it might contain could be far more important. "A witch device? Built by the Adversaries?"

The Navigator shook his head impatiently, wishing that his Order's prohibitions against scientific inquiry had not resulted in such widespread ignorance and superstition. "Built by men, Glamiss. Imperials."

"How long ago?"

"I don't know," the Navigator said. "No one does."

Glamiss's eyes narrowed speculatively. "It answers questions?"

"I think it does much more. But it does give answers—"

"To those who know how to ask, is that it?" Glamiss was studying the lightened panel before them. "You say there is a thing like this in the Cloister?"

"Something like it."

"Did you ever speak to it?"

"I'm only a priest-Nav, a starship pilot. No one below the rank of Bishop ever got near the thing."

"But you know the *theory*?"

"All Navigators do. It's part of the third year's teaching of the Way."

"Then ask it how old it is," Glamiss said.

The Rhadan flexed his fingers and looked hard at the panel. Below the lighted buttons was a keyboard. The symbols were Imperial Anglic—the holy language. If God in the Star had not wanted a Navigator to deal with this device, surely he would not have written the keyboard in the holy script?

He pressed the query key.

Nothing happened.

"What's the matter?" Glamiss asked.

Emeric shook his head impatiently. "Let me think." He studied the panel again, more carefully. At the head of the column of keys were two oddly shaped rocker switches. They were marked STANDBY and ACTIVATE. The standby rocker was depressed. He touched the mate and the standby switch popped to the neutral position. A series of lights appeared across the border of the panel and a section of the wall in front of the egg retracted, exposing a blue-lighted screen. Emeric's mouth felt dry. The screen was like the dead screens in the bridge of a starship.

Again he pressed the query button and this time a light stylus seemed to write across the screen. The word was simply: *Ready*.

"The thing recognizes you," Glamiss said, hiding his own rising excitement behind ironic words.

Emeric, pecking slowly at the keyboard, posed a question: "When were you built?"

Instantly the reply appeared on the screen, and simultaneously on a strip of plastic tape that extruded from a slit in the panel like a white tongue. A date: *2920 GE*. A pause, then two more dates appeared below the original light inscription: *9520 AD* and *611 P*.

The two young men stared at the glowing numbers. The Galactic Era had begun with the foundation of the Empire. This machine had been built 2,920 years later, when the Empire was already in decline. The thought was awesome. The accepted date used now for the current year, Emeric thought, was *3946 GE*. But there was no one who could say with certainty that it was a *correct* date, relative to the founding of the Empire, because no one was certain how long the time of troubles and the Dark Age had lasted. Navigator astronomers were prohibited from making the necessary observations by the Inquisition.

"What are the other dates?" Glamiss asked.

"The AD stands for Anno Domini—The Year of Our Lord. Dawn Age dating. No one is absolutely certain who Our Lord was, but we assume he was a religious figure. The P date is years from the official date of the first colony founded on the planet. Local dating."

"This place is a thousand years old?" Glamiss asked in disbelief. "And it still functions?"

"So it would seem, Glamiss Warleader," the priest said, half disbelieving it himself.

"Ask it, to be certain," Glamiss demanded. " 'How old are you—in standard years.' Ask it that."

Before Emeric could type out the question, the lights winked swiftly and on the screen there appeared the figure *4,117 SY*.

"Four thousand years? That's impossible. It misunderstood me." Glamiss said.

The Navigator stared thoughtfully at the numbers and presently he shook his head. "It didn't misunderstand you, Glamiss. Computers don't. Our history is wrong. The dark years have lasted longer than anyone imagines. Our dates are all incorrect; the Civil Wars were so horrible men even lost track of the time they spent in barbarism." He studied his friend in a new, bleaker light. If Glamiss's dreams should become reality, if they took the form of a holy war of reconquest, didn't men run the risk of another bloodbath followed by an even darker night?

Glamiss, unmindful of his friend's scrutiny, was characteristically plunging on, exploiting this new and miraculous source of information.

"What is this place?"

"Medical records library," the screen flashed promptly.

"No, I mean *all* this place. The mountain. Everything."

"You are in the Imperial Cryonics Hospital, Aldrin," the computer replied.

"Aldrin?"

"That is the Imperial name for this planet, Glamiss," Emeric murmured. "The old man—the Warlock—he used it, remember?"

"Let's find out about *him*," Glamiss said. "List what you know about—" He turned to Emeric. "what was the name the Voice used?"

"Ophir," the Navigator said.

Lines of print appeared swiftly on the screen. Glamiss said, "Read it out, Emeric. My Anglic isn't good enough."

The Navigator translated the symbols on the screen with a growing sense of wonder.

"The Right Honorable Ophir ben Rigell ibn Sol alt Messier. Cryonic patient Number A7-1998-65008 Special Category. Entered ICH Aldrin 10-3-3550, Cryonized 10-26-3550. Diagnosis: Trilaudid addiction with associated blindness, psychedelic disturbances, hypertension, cellular edema and schizo-paranoia. More detailed information can be obtained from Special Category File on presentation of Need-To-Know security credentials relating to Imperial Family."

Glamiss's mind rocked with the inevitable implications of what the devil machine was telling them. The old Warlock *was* a man of the Golden Age. And he was not just *any* man, but an alt Messier Rigellian, closely related to the last Galacton of the Empire, Rigell XXVIII!

"What is this *cryonization*, Emeric," Glamiss asked in a hoarse whisper, as though fearful the machine would overhear.

"It is a term that appears in the legends of the Golden Age, Glamiss," the priest whispered back as hoarsely. "It is an abomination of Sin and Cyb. Living men were frozen, preserved in an icy hell for all eternity."

"Stop it, man," Glamiss said sharply. "It must have been a thing men did either to punish other men—or—" He had a sudden insight into the nature of this place now. It was, the computer had said, a *hospital*. People were sent here to be cured, or cared for. Not to be damned and tortured. And if that unbelievable old man was, indeed, who the machine said he was, he would have had the finest medical care available in that time of miracles.

"Explain cryonization," he demanded of the computer.

There followed a torrent of incomprehensible symbols and formulae. Useless. "Stop!" Glamiss ordered. He rephrased his question. "Why are people cryonized?"

"Patients are cryonized in the hope that they can be preserved in a medically inert state until research discovers specific treatments for their complaints." Pause. "However, there is a limit to the time a human body can be preserved with extreme cold. This limit varies with individuals, but is generally believed to be between 3,000 and 4,000 standard years depending on age, weight, heredity, and other factors. When the limit time is in danger of being exceeded, the cryonized patient is revived regardless of the state of the art relative to his disease. This is Imperial medical policy."

Filled with a sense of unreality at this peculiar conversation, Glamiss asked: "The old man—the Lord Ophir—can he be cured of whatever is wrong with him?"

"No. There has been no research on the trilaudid addiction syndrome since 3565 GE, and no medical research of any kind since 3610 GE. Lord Ophir will die."

There it was, Glamiss thought bitterly. They had stumbled onto a mountain of miracles, but the only living human being who could truly understand them and tell him how these miracles might be used was dying. Blind, drug-addicted, now injured by the idiot attack from the sky, the old man might at this moment be breathing his last.

Emeric, the Rhadan noble, had veered off on another line of inquiry. He was asking the machine, "Is the Lord Ophir a Rhad?"

"Technically, no, he is not. Members of the Imperial Family are all by law considered citizens of Earth, Sol III. However, Lord Ophir was born on Rhada and bears the title of Prince of that colony. It is his personal holding as King-Elector and Heir."

For an instant Glamiss forgot that the Navigator and the machine were discussing matters millennia out of date. He had heard the words "King-Elector" and "Heir."

"That old man is the legal heir to Rigell?"

"Unless the Galacton has remarried and fathered sons not registered in the ICH data bank," came the reply. Glamiss suppressed an impulse to break into foolish laughter. He had been right about the machine having been built by men and not by the Adversaries. Only a device constructed by men— clever, but essentially brainless—would fail to understand that the world it was discussing was dust.

But the old man was legal heir to the Empire. *That* was a bit of information worth having. Had fate, and his own weakness for drugs, not struck him down—*he might have died wearing the feathered cape and carrying the golden flail of Empire*—

The irony of the moment bid fair to overwhelm him. He remained silent for a long while as Emeric, his Nav's brain hungry for knowledge, plied the machine with questions. Now Glamiss's mind was elsewhere. He was thinking of the blind old man dying among strangers, deserted by his retreating people millennia ago. *That*, the young warleader thought, was the stuff of true loneliness. Abandoned not only by your *kind*, but by your *time* as well . . .

He was still deep in thought when he heard the call that Ulm's first waves were attacking up the moraine.

Chapter Fourteen

Saint and King together, within the fabled Mountain
Guarded the Immortal who held the Sacred Key to
Nyor. A thousand warmen waited, ten thousand more
a-coming, Under the black and silken banners.

> —Guest Song, Early Second Stellar
> Empire period

If the engagement some historians call the Battle of
Trama was ever actually fought (which is doubtful),
our accounts of it are (to say the least) meager. Secular
historians have suggested that the so-called battle was
provoked by a Bishop of the Order of Navigators allied
with the local warlord. They have further implied that
the Order was determined to destroy the mysterious
"Mountain of Trama" rather than permit the benefits
of its First Empire science to reach the commonality of
Vyka. The facts do not support these canards.

> —Nav (Bishop) Julianus Mullerium,
> *Anticlericalism in the Age of the
> Star Kings,* Middle Second Stellar
> Empire period

Bishop-Navigator Kaifa, sitting on the broad back of an ill-tempered black mare from Ulm's stables, watched the disorganized milling about of the Vara-Vykan levy with growing impatience.

The men had taken an hour or more to alight from the starship and immediately had scattered to loot the hovels of the abandoned village of Trama—though what they could possibly find there that was worth stealing the Navigator could not imagine, so poor was the settlement.

The indiscipline of the Varan warmen was more than simply irritating to Kaifa. It was undermining his confidence in the course of action he had now set in motion.

A Navigator of Bishop's rank was, to all intents and purposes, an independent agent in the far space of the Rimworlds. By his actions he could affect the political course of events almost at will. And if he were successful—that is, if the results benefited the Order—he would be reckoned accountable to no one, even his superiors within the hierarchy of the Order.

But if his choices were indiscreet—if the results were unsatisfactory to the grim old men who surrounded the Grand Master—retribution could be swift and terrible.

The Order's computer in Algol had warned of a politico-historical nexus forming on Vyka. It had remembered a forgotten concentration of imperial science within the mountain overlooking the valley of Trama. The decision had been to strike a bargain with Lord Ulm for ecclesiastical sovereignty over Trama. Kaifa frowned. Had it really been *the* decision? Or did it stand, in the records of the Holy Order of Navigators, as *Bishop Kaifa's* decision?

He looked about him at the barbarian rabble that was Ulm's army. Of all the men who had served the dropsical Lord of Vara-Vyka, only young Glamiss had commanded a disciplined and trained force. This distinction had cost him dearly—for the jealous men who surrounded Ulm had convinced the Lord of Trama-Vyka that he nurtured a traitor in Glamiss.

But though Kaifa was a worldly man, he was still a priest and dedicated to the real and eternal mission of his Order: to preserve knowledge and to form an island in the barbaric sea that was the Great Sky.

Had he backed the wrong man? That was the question that gnawed at his conscience and his confidence.

The warleader Linne, a hulking and black-visaged brute of a man, was cantering along the front of forming companies, cursing and beating men into position with the butt of his flail. In time, Kaifa thought, Linne would be exactly like Ulm was now: gross, brutal, and self-indulgent. It seemed very probable that Ulm, having discarded his youngest and most able warleader Glamiss and all the warmen loyal to him, had stripped himself of whatever defense he might soon need against Linne, who would undoubtedly take Vara-Vyka when this fight was over and the starship gone.

That, the Navigator thought bitterly, was the recurring pattern of life among the lords of the Great Sky. Cruelty, repression, treachery, and revolt. Again and again he had seen it, and he sometimes wondered about the Order's notion that simply by monopolizing and protecting the remnants of Empire science they could one day insure a rebirth of Community. Wasn't it just possible that the Order was wrong? That the only thing that would recreate the Empire was a *secular* conqueror? It was a thought dangerously close to heresy, but Kaifa had studied what history existed and he knew that Man, even long before he left Earth for the stars, had proved himself volatile and aggressive. What refinement Man had achieved had always been paid for in blood. Those who spoke of love and brotherhood were those lucky enough to be born in a time of Man's rest from his labors; the predators had let it be safe, for a time, to be weak. And then, inevitably, the wheel of history turned and the weak were crushed while the warriors carved another cave of refuge from a hostile universe.

Kaifa brushed these disturbing thoughts aside and stared up at the level place at the head of the moraine. Glamiss's troopers now made not the slightest effort to hide themselves or their intentions. They would fight—and the ground favored them. Mere numbers would not dislodge them.

Again, Kaifa cursed the momentary carelessness that had allowed Ulm's orders for bombardment from the air to be carried out. To stone warriors in such a situation had been folly. And the final responsibility had been his own. His brain fuddled with strategy, he had neglected simple tactics. Now Glamiss held the mountain and all it contained, and for an assault force there was only the rabble of Vara-Vyka.

Linne had formed the first troop of the levy in the moraine. The war mares screamed angrily, sensing the nearness of battle. The Bishops's own mount growled and turned her head to glare at her rider, her fanged mouth open and salivating.

"Stand, damn you," Kaifa said, crossly.

"We go. We fight," the mare said.

Kaifa cuffed her across the ears. *"Stand!"* Bloody Rhadan beast. They were near to unmanageable for anyone not trained to ride them. The thought came to him that the young priest with Glamiss was a Rhadan—a noble Rhad, in fact. More trouble for the Order when all this was done, Kaifa thought. Events were like a skein unraveling, tangling. Who could foresee the eventual results of this grubby skirmish in the wilds of a backward fief on a wilderness Rimworld? He shivered with unaccustomed apprehension.

He urged his mount closer to the disorganized rabble milling about in their attempt to form ranks in the confining space of the moraine. As he did so, he was dismayed to see a party of what appeared to be villagers driving a small herd of weyr into the mountain under the protection of the rebel warmen's crossbows and javelins.

He rode to Ulm's side and pointed them out. The lord of Vara-Vyka was sweating heavily in his armor and his breathing was hard and labored. He was taking no part in organizing the attack, leaving it all to Linne and the other warleaders.

Kaifa pointed out the foraging party and said irritably, "Can't you do something to stop that? We'll never starve them out if all those weyr get into the mountain."

"I have no intention of making a siege, Holy Father," the lord of Vara said stupidly. "Let them stuff the mountain with weyr. It won't save the rebels."

Kaifa chewed his lips in exasperation. In a controlled voice he pointed out that taking the rebel position by assault might be impossible. "A dozen men can hold that tunnel-mouth," he said.

Ulm's glistening face worked dully, his piggish eyes squinting against the glare of the yellowish sunlight. "Now, My Lord Bishop, starships and religion are your business. Fighting is mine. Be content."

Kaifa stared bleakly at the confusion of the levy—a thousand troopers scattered between the moraine and the starship in the meadow below. Some of the warmen were still rooting about in the village, looking for loot. He was filled with angry despair. The whole affair was turning into a fiasco—from the ill-considered stoning from the air to this—this disorganized mob-scene.

"They will make guest songs of this," Ulm said fatuously. "People will remember the battle of Trama."

Bishop Kaifa trembled with the effort of suppressing his fury. He looked longingly up at the mountain thinking of the imperial wonders it must contain. All just out of his reach. All, he thought bleakly, available to young Emeric Kiersson-Rhad. Great Star, what ironies there were in life.

He thought suddenly of the hot sands of his native Nasser, of the blazing sky of the galactic center, and of the noble, lonely life of his Bedouin ancestors. Thirty years' service to the Order had brought him to this place and the tools crumbled in his hands. Ulm, Linne, and the others were too dull, too stupid even to guess at the importance of what was happening here. But it was too late to change the course of events now. The Algol computer had directed that all this should happen and so it must. But the Order, Bishop Kaifa thought, the *Order* must be protected against failure—against the results of faulty decisions made by a probably faulty machine. He raised his eyes to the yellow star blazing in the clear sky. The Star. God. Allah. Men gave many names to the spirit of the Universe. But it was *there*, always. And computers or no, the Order of Navigators was a *religious* order, and as a servant of God one must have faith. He closed his eyes and said aloud the words he had learned as a child, even before his Selection for the Holy Order; the words of the ancient Book of Nasser, the Koran: *"As for him who performeth a good work, verily Allah is grateful and knowing."*

The first wave of Ulm's men had begun to gallop to the attack up the boulder-strewn steepness of the moraine.

* * *

With a dozen men ranked behind him on the ferroconcrete platform, Glamiss waited for the assault. His eyes were cold and steady as he watched Ulm's warmen straggle up the steepening slope. He knew many of the attackers; they had been his friends in Ulm's service. But they were not his friends now, and he gave a quiet order to his crossbowmen.

He held his hand steadily raised.

He saw Linne Warleader in the first row of horsemen. Very brave, Glamiss thought icily, and very foolish. To attack a position like this one with a cavalry charge was what he would have expected from Linne and Ulm. There would be widows in Vara keep tonight, Glamiss thought bleakly.

He dropped his hand and the air thrummed with quarrels. The charge broke up a dozen meters from the platform. Mares shrieked, clawing at the air. Men spilled from their saddles and fell back upon their fellows. Glamiss saw a dark face turn crimson, a sword spin high in the air, red-smeared at the hilt where a quarrel had mashed a hand and fingers.

He raised his hand again. Lowered it. The air hummed once more with iron missiles. Now the charge was folding back upon itself, tumbling back like a river of flesh and iron, down the moraine.

Then Ulm's soldiers were retreating—those left alive. There were a score of men and a half dozen mares among the boulders of the slope. Some lay still—others twitched and jerked, still others crawled down the gouge in the ground left by the retreating glacier, leaving a red trail behind them.

"A pity to kill good horses," a warmen said behind Glamiss.

The warleader did not turn. He did not want his men to see the gray bleakness in his face. A waste, he was thinking, a senseless brutal *waste*. Men should die for something. Not like this, for the Red Fist and Ulm's dull-witted jealousy.

He glanced at the sun. Hours until darkness. Time for a dozen of these hopeless, bloody attacks. Earlier he had looked forward to the test of battle. But now, seeing the dead in the moraine and the wounded crawling over the red-smeared stones, he hated the sight and smell of fighting.

"They're coming again, Glamiss Warleader."

He saw that they were, Linne's hulking strength once again in the lead.

Glamiss felt a chill satisfaction. Stupid, yes. But there were no cowards on Vyka.

The crossbows were reloaded with the last of the quarrels. The next charge would be met with javelins, and then the next hand to hand, blade against blade. It would be a long, terrible afternoon, Glamiss knew, and victory—if it came—would be bitter.

Chapter Fifteen

Unhallowed knowledge brought the Dark Time . . .
So I say this to you: Seek not to know, for to know is to
sin . . . . He who disturbs the mysterious ways of the
Universe is heretic, and enemy of God and Man. *And he
will burn.*

> —Talvas Hu Chien, Grand Master and Grand
> Inquisitor of Navigators, Interregnal
> period

When the end came, it came very swiftly. Dissent led
to revolution, revolution to anarchy, anarchy to the rule
of warlords. The Empire quite literally *imploded*, collapsing under the pressure of revolt on the frontiers.
Rigell XXVIII died in the rubble of atom-blasted Nyor,
surrounded by his drug- and pleasure-enfeebled nobility. They died like sheep.

One exception was The Right Honorable Lady Dihanna alt Aldrin, Mistress of Vega. She gathered a small
force and attempted to fight her way back to Aldrin. It
has been suggested that her intention was to collect the
galactic Heir, said to be in seclusion on Aldrin, but

this is unproven. The Lady Dihanna's squadron was en-
globed by the starships of the Revolutionary Dictator-
ship of Canopus near the Horsehead and wiped out,
effectively ending any hope of a Restoration of the
Rigellian hegemony.
          —Matthias ben Mullerium, *The Decline and Fall.*
          of the First Stellar Empire, Late Second
          Stellar Empire period

Navigator Emeric of Rhada rubbed his burning eyes and
read on. He had been at it for hours now, and the glittering
letters that flashed across the cathode ray screen of the library
computer seemed to dance and skitter about in his head. But
still he kept at it, his Nav-trained mind hungry for knowledge.

The computer's programming had ended, he understood
now, at a point in time (he no longer cared how long ago it was
in years) when the Empire was actually in the process of collapsing. The Outer Marches were in revolt, Imperial military
and police units were mutinying, "people's militias" were dis-
pensing summary "justice" throughout the Rimworlds, and
the social services that meant the difference between civilization and barbarism were collapsing.

He felt worn and light-headed from fatigue and hunger, but
the pulsing flow of information from the computer seemed to
sustain him like a drug; he would pay the price of it later, but
for now he could not drink the torrent of facts fast enough.

He had, in the time since Glamiss had left him to organize
the defense of the hospital, managed to piece together a number of fascinating bits about the hospital itself and the cryonized patients who had once filled it to overflowing.

The hedonistic culture of the late empire had created a
whole class of drug-addicted nobility. Trilaudid and other
"mind-expanders" had come into general usage among the
Imperial aristocracy before the pleasure-seeking nobles and
their medics had learned the potential side-effects—one of
which was blindness.

The unspoken but clear purpose of the hospital on Aldrin
was to preserve the drug-addicted aristocrats (out of the

public's view) until medical science could correct the damage they had done themselves.

The revolution and civil wars had interrupted any hope of this. Even during the time included in the computer's programming, cryonized patients were being removed to other hospitals nearer the galactic center where they would be safe from the People's Armies that were spreading terror and destruction through the Rimworld regions.

Lord Ophir, the computer seemed to be saying, remained in his cryonic capsule to the end. It appeared that the hospital staff had been instructed by the liege of Aldrin, one Lady alt Aldrin, to remain with the King-Elector's frozen body until relieved.

It was obvious that the expected relief had never come and the doctors had finally deserted the hospital and its single, most-royal patient.

Emeric leaned back in the contour chair and squeezed the bridge of his nose wearily. He was unbelievably tired, but the machine had opened up a fantastic window into the distant past—the imperial world of great lords and ladies and men who ruled—not nations and holdings—but star systems. The Age of the first Star Kings.

He had uncovered one other piece of knowledge—*dangerous* knowledge. Glamiss had come into the mountain hoping to find weapons. The discovery that the caves were part of a hospital complex had persuaded him that there were no weapons. But Glamiss's assumption had been wrong. The computer had printed out a map of the hospital for the Navigator, and it contained indications that there was a small armory in the depths of the mountain. Emeric absorbed this information with dismay, though not with great surprise. Any place protecting an imperial personage would certainly have weapons for its security forces. The Navigator hoped fervently that the other vanished imperials, the human doctors and cyborg attendants, had taken the weapons with them when they fled.

But the thought of the magically terrible imperial weapons (Emeric could only guess at their capabilities) stirred an even deeper fear. He queried the computer once again: "How is this place kept functioning all the time?" He had a dreadful feeling that the reply would come as no real surprise. The libraries on Algol contained much information on the nature of imperial power plants.

The computer flashed the words: "Nuclear power."

Emeric shivered and punched out: "Expand reply."

There followed in swift succession a half-dozen sets of plans and schematics detailing the location and capacity of the thermonuclear pile on which the mountain rested.

Emeric made the sign of the Star and bit his lips. Atomics. Naturally. What else could keep this complexity of services and machines operating through millenia?

It was as though the mountain itself had opened, spread batlike wings, and assumed the aspect of sharp-snouted Sin Himself: the dark Adversary.

Vulk Asa found him in an attitude of prayer.

"Nav Emeric."

The Rhadan looked up bleakly. "What is it?"

"The Warlock wants to speak with you, Lord."

Emeric rubbed a hand across his eyes. "With me?"

"He is dying, Nav."

For a moment Emeric was overwhelmed with a sense of the terrible death the old Imperial faced: blind, drug-destroyed, and so dreadfully *alone*; an anachronism thousands of years displaced from his proper locus in the great panorama of history.

A Navigator had duties and obligations to the dying. It was part of the Way.

"I'll come," he said, and left the computer terminal reluctantly, but with a sense of returning to his own proper place in time.

It was the darkness that finally convinced Lord Ophir it was time to give up the struggle. As long as the radar-electronic prosthesis implanted in his shoulder brought him images of the outside world, life—even the nightmare life he now lived— was worth *something*.

But a stone—a *stone*, by all the stars!—had fallen from the air and smashed his eyes and his body, and now he no longer wished to live in this barbaric dreamland of a future.

Strangely enough, his injury and the destruction of the mechanisms of his robe seemed to have liberated him from his slavery to trilaudid. His body still craved the drug, but the failure of the machines with which the hospital computer had kept him alive had reduced his physical awareness to the level of near-senility. He could no longer want anything very much: not drugs, not sight or warmth or food or—finally—even life.

He could sense the nearness of the barbarian girl, Shana. She had materialized in his blind darkness, and he could feel her near him now. He could smell her, too, he thought, wrinkling his nose with aristocratic fastidiousness. She moved in an effluvium of badly-tanned animal skins and unwashed young flesh.

He felt like talking. The pity was that he could only talk *at* the girl, and not *to* her. Too many centuries separated the center line of their respective lives. Still, knowing how near death was, he made the effort.

"Shana?"

"I'm here, Lord."

The Warlock laughed inwardly, soundlessly, baring his yellow teeth. "Are the eagles flying, Shana?"

"Yea, Lord. I tried to make them attack the warmen, but they are frightened now, after what Glamiss Warleader did to them in the meadow."

"It's well," he said.

Shana frowned. "Well, Lord?"

"Men should fight their own battles." He muttered heavily in Imperial Anglic and Shana asked, "What did you say, Lord?"

"Don't call me that," he said in dialect.

"You are a great lord, a great Warlock." The girl no longer believed it, but she, too, knew he was dying and she did not wish to be disrespectful.

"I have only one claim to uniqueness left," the Warlock said. "I am the oldest living trilaudid addict." He laughed brokenly.

Shana did not know what to reply and so remained silent.

He lay on a pallet, his silver robe dull and inert. The nutrient tank in the far corner of the luxurious room rippled softly—like the river, Shana thought. Like the river at moons-rise.

"There is something I want done," Ophir said. "Where is that Vulk?"

"He has gone for the priest, Lord."

"The priest, is it?" The old man giggled softly. "I'm to have the comforts of religion, am I?"

"It is the Way of the Navigators to comfort the dying when they can," Shana said practically. Death was a common thing, a part of life. She felt no reticence in mentioning it.

"How civilized," Ophir said. "In my day, we were not so considerate." He remembered the plots and counterplots surrounding the monarchy. Nyor had been a golden death-trap, a fortress, a prison for all Rigellians. Perhaps that was why he had turned to trilaudid—for the illusion of freedom. But what did it matter now?

Suddenly the computer spoke through the speaker grille. "Please enter your nutrient bath, Lord Ophir. Your robe is inoperative. If you do not comply, a cyborg will be sent."

"Idiot machine," Ophir murmured, grinning like a death's head. "There are no cybs left."

Shana felt a chill at the mention of the dreadful word *Cyb*. Unseen, she made the sign of the Star and whispered an Ave Stella.

Ophir said, "Don't be frightened, girl. The cybs are all gone—gone forever." He had found the remains of only three in all the empty hospital: withered androgynes, half-machine, half-human, but totally dead, their flesh mummified by the cool dry air of centuries.

"Shana—have you ever been off-world?" the Warlock asked.

"Oh, no, Lord," the girl replied. Didn't the old man realize that such adventures were only for nobles or Navigators or possibly warriors? No, of course he did not. In that mysterious place whence he had come, many went out among the stars of the Great Sky.

"I would have liked to see Rhada again," he said.

"The Nav is a Rhadan," Shana said.

"Tell me about the—Nav."

"I cannot, Lord. I know nothing." She paused thoughtfully. "He wears the Fist, but I think he is kind—for a great lord, that is."

"Great lords are not kind, are they?" The Warlock seemed to find this amusing. "They never have been, Shana. That's why they are great lords."

"If you say so, Lord."

"Tell me what the Nav does."

Shana frowned. What could he be thinking of? Everyone knew what Navigators did. "They own the starships, Lord."

"So," Ophir murmured. "Well, why not? It's all happened before. Ten thousand years ago, the Church kept the light burning."

"I do not understand, Lord."

"There is no reason why you should, child." Suddenly it seemed terribly important to him—that *history* should not die completely in *this* dark age. The Vulk know, he thought, but the Vulk are aliens, they are not men. And they keep their own counsel for Vulkish reasons Man might never understand. No, the fragile links of history were *human* links. So must it ever be.

He heard a chink of iron mail and the rustle of homespun. Shana said, "The Nav is here, Lord."

The Vulk, as well, Ophir thought. Perhaps it was his drug-altered mind's strange sensitivity, but he could *feel* the alien nearby, and the Vulk knew it. There was an aura in the room that had not been there before: kindness, yes, and compassion and a strange, untouchable alienation. And an unbelievable *patience*. We are old, we two, the Warlock thought and he felt that the Vulk read his thought and agreed.

"Navigator," Ophir said, "do I know your name?"

"I am Emeric Kiersson-Rhad, Warlock."

Ophir smiled to himself at that. Warlock. Witches. Men with swords sweeping across the galaxy at a thousand times the speed of light. Did they have any notion of the wonders they had inherited from the shattered Empire, he wondered with Rigellian pride. Empty pride, he cautioned himself. My world is dead and I am dying—while they, ignorant and crude, are strong and young and alive.

"Shana, leave us now," the Warlock said.

The girl looked at the Navigator for permission and he

nodded. When she was gone, Vulk Asa said, "Shall I leave you, too?"

"No," the Warlock said. "We have no secrets from one another, we two."

Emeric looked sharply at Asa, but the featureless face was unreadable. Vulkish ways, Emeric thought with a twinge of prejudice. Who could understand them?

"You, priest," the Warlock said, "you are what passes for a scientist in this benighted time?"

Emeric bit his lip at the obscene word "scientist." But he said, "I am a Guide of Starships, Warlock."

"That counts for something, I suppose," Ophir said, with a touch of his ancient arrogance. "Have you been idle here?"

"I found the medical library and the computer terminal, if that is what you wish to know," Emeric said.

"Good, sir priest. Very *good*. In my day religious fanatics were not so enlightened. Then not all science is forgotten, I take it? You still use computers?"

"There is one in all the Great Sky." He was tempted to add that the data banks had been tampered with many times in Algol, but he did not wish to denigrate the princes of his Order, and so said nothing.

"I am dying," the Warlock said.

"Yes," Emeric said mercilessly. Like Shana, he was accustomed to death. It was simply a reality of this dark age. It came in many forms, most of them violent, and here was a man who had clearly lived a very long time. The Warlock had no real cause for complaint. The spirit of God in the Star had been kinder to him than most.

"You are a Rhadan."

"Yes. Of the Northern Rhad."

"Tell me of our world, priest. I should like to hear. Is it still beautiful?"

Emeric essayed a half-smile. "The sea is still blue-green. It still turns to silver when the winds come from the polar north. The plains are a sea of grass and one may still see the wind as it blows."

"The mountains?"

"Timbered still. The snow remains until mid-summer in the high passes. There are not many of us—"

"There never were," the Warlock said, with evident satisfaction. "I am glad men haven't made it into a rabbit-warren. They did that to the Inner Worlds, you know, long ago."

"I know—Lord Ophir."

"You know who I am, then. Yes, of course. The computer—"

"I do not know that I believe it—with my head. But in my belly I feel it is true. I don't understand it well, but it must be so."

The Warlock asked softly, "Would all Navigators be that open-minded, priest?"

"I doubt it. Who could blame them?"

Ophir laughed thinly, his shallow breath wheezing. "Who, indeed?"

The old man fell silent for a time, then he said, "I was struck by a stone from a starship. Did I imagine that?"

"No. There are warmen outside this place attacking."

The mention of an attack did not faze the Warlock, but he said wonderingly, "*Stones*. Dropped from starships." He drew a breath with difficulty. "I feel almost no pain. Perhaps if I were younger I might survive this injury, but I am not —and I no longer care to go on—for reasons that you may shortly know, priest."

Emeric remained respectfully silent.

"You are a savage, sir priest. But you are the nearest thing to a civilized man on Aldrin—" There was a slight emphasis on the word "man" that Emeric did not miss. Vulk Asa remained impassive, not wishing—or so it seemed—to interfere in a human matter. "Therefore I am going to ask that you take a risk."

"A risk?"

"Did the idiot computer inform you about personality transfer therapy?"

"No."

"Probably because it never worked. It was intended to achieve some sort of psychic balance between two minds. All it ever really did was produce some idiot-savants and transfer more information that even a computer can process." He became agitated and turned to search for Emeric with his blind eyes. "You say you know who I am?"

"Yes. You are—were—the King-Elector."

"Your choice of tense is correct. Now, tell me, is there a man in the galaxy who knows what I know of man's past?"

"Unless there were other places like this one, there is not," the Navigator said.

The Warlock's tone grew slightly crafty. "Would you like to know what I know, priest? *All* that I know? Every bit, every fact, *all*?"

"There isn't time."

"A lifetime wouldn't be long enough to *teach* you. You are a barbarian. You haven't the basic knowledge."

Emeric's heart began to beat more heavily. He could sense that he was going to be tested, and tested, perhaps, beyond the power of mortal man to withstand.

The Warlock went on swiftly now. "There is danger, I won't deny you that. I'm a triaudid addict. My sanity comes and goes. If it goes while we are attempting a personality transfer, it could destroy your reason. I am dying. If I should die while the probes connect us, I don't know what would happen to you. Because what I am suggesting, priest, is that we connect our minds by machine—and when it is done you will have all the knowledge that my forebrain contains. *All of it*." He laughed with a sudden, alarming wildness. "That will make you a saint or a madman, Emeric Kiersson-Rhad. Do you know the Faust legend? No? Well, never mind—if you have the courage, *you will*."

Emeric's mouth felt dry. "You can do this thing?" He scarcely dared free his mind to imagine the possession of such knowledge and powers.

"I can. With your help."

"Why? Why should you want to?" Emeric could not suppress the tiny bead of suspicion that had formed in his chest—a feeling, no more.

"I'm not an altruist," the Warlock said. "But you see that I am old—I am dying. Say only that dying men make strange bequests. I am a learned man, priest. I offer you knowledge." He struggled to rise and did manage to push himself up so that his seamed face confronted both the Vulk and Emeric.

His voice was strong, impossibly strong and clear. *"And*

knowledge is power, Emeric of Rhada. Are you man enough to take it?''

The words meant something else, Emeric sensed that. But the prize was too great to let fear command him.

''Tell me how this thing can be done,'' Emeric said.

Only Vulk Asa sensed the presence of the girl Shana listening beside the open door in the passageway. He heard her run swiftly and knew that she was frightened and was seeking Glamiss to tell him what his chaplain now planned to do.

Chapter Sixteen

You shall know the truth, and the truth shall enslave
all mankind.

> —From *The Book of Warls,*
> Interregnal period.

The young, in their self-righteousness, claim that
there is no past. The old, in their bitterness, claim that
there is no future. But the wise, young *and* old, know
that the past unlocks the future, and that those who
scorn the history of the race or its posterity are fools. I
make no special claim to wisdom: My awakening was by
chance. For one terrible moment, I clasped hands with
both future and past.

> —*The Dialogues of St. Emeric,* Early
> Second Stellar Empire period.

The main entrance tunnel was crowded with men, some
wounded, some resting, some even sleeping, battle-exhausted.
There were villagers, as well, Tamil Hind for one, herding
bleating weyr deeper into the mountain. And overall there

hung the smell of battle: of sweaty men and sweetish blood and oiled iron. Shana shoved her way impatiently toward the fading light of day she could see the tunnel mouth, seeking Glamiss the Warleader.

Tamil said, "Here, Shana! Where are you going? You can't go out there—they're slaughtering one another." His voice implied that this was fine with him, that these intruders in the valley should be allowed to butcher one another to the end, leaving things as they were before they came. Shana, who was not a fool as Tamil was, knew that things would never again be the same in Trama. The very sky had fallen on the village and its people, and it was senseless to dream of what could never be again.

Tamil caught her arm and said, "Shana, didn't you hear me?"

Shana pulled away from him and said, "Don't start getting brave *now*, Tamil." She drew the knife-that-burns from under her weyr skins and held it. She had taken it from the Warlock, for it was a sacred talisman of the village, and in the confusion she had managed to retrieve it. "Last night you were willing to let them use this on me. Why are you so concerned about my safety now?"

Tamil stood crestfallen. "These are bad times, Shana," he muttered.

"Then herd the weyr inside and let me be. Or times will get worse." She turned away and hurried on past the warmen and the crowding villagers.

When she reached the tunnel mouth and could look down the slope of the moraine, she was appalled by what she saw. Dead and wounded men and horses clogged the stony defile. Two kilometers away she could see the humped back of the great starship. Its immense weight had made a depression in the meadow and men on war mares milled about the mystical shape in seemingly confused excitement.

A number of warmen were returning to the concrete platform from the moraine after a sharp skirmish that had, apparently, sent still another detachment of Lord Ulm's men retreating down the mountain toward the village. At the head of the battle-stained and weary troop walked the young man they called Glamiss. His reddened, naked sword was in his hands, and his bare arms were stained below the edge of his mailed sleeves.

Somehow, in spite of her antagonism, she was strangely stirred by the sight of him. He carried himself like a lord, even though her woman's eye told her that he was sore and very weary.

He caught sight of her and essayed a grim smile that seemed to light up his grimy face. "Have you come to see the fighting, then, Shana, daughter of Shevaughn Six-fingers?"

"This is stupid," the girl said smartly.

"Oh?" He was on the platform now, looking down on her. She could see that he was unwounded, and for some reason it eased her mind that he had not been hurt.

"Yes," she said. "Ulm's men can't get in. But we can't get out, either. Nothing gained and nothing lost—except men. How many have been killed?" Her voice was edged with bitterness, because she understood that killing was the business of soldiers, yet it was horrible that it must always be so.

Glamiss's expression became somber. "I have lost a dozen good warriors."

"And Ulm?"

His voice was steely. "Three times that."

"Half a hundred dead or wounded." Shana shivered. "They would have been better born to herd weyr or to plant grain."

Glamiss sheathed his great sword and put his hands heavily on Shana's narrow shoulders. "That is the Star's truth, girl. I wish no man's death in battle. It's an empty business."

"You believe that?" she asked, surprised.

"I believe it," he said heavily. "But until *all* men believe it, you must have order. And most men want order imposed only on others. It is the way of the world, Shana-the-hetman's-daughter," he finished, almost tenderly rallying her.

For a moment her senses reeled with the sudden warmth and power of his personality. She had the crazy notion that she, if he would only ask it of her, would follow him willingly across the Great Sky. Part of it was that he was an attractive and virile young man—really not so much older than herself. But there was more: Glamiss was obviously gifted with the power to command loyalty—even from those who had no notion of his purposes, who might actually lose by his attainment of them.

She drew a quick breath and remembered why she had sought him out. "Your friend, the Navigator," she said, "you should go to him."

"Emeric? Why? I'm needed here."

"How can I say this?" she asked, perplexed. "I know that you must stop what the Warlock is going to do to him—"

"The old man, Shana? Why he's dying, girl. And in any case, Emeric could snuff him out like a candle-flame."

Shana shook her head stubbornly. "I stood by the door and listened. The old man—" she did not think of him as "lord" any longer—"is tricking him. He's promising him strange *knowledge*—" She caught at Glamiss's wrist, feeling the strength of it under her hand. "There are terrible machines in this place, Glamiss, I *know*. I'm an adept. I've glimpsed things in the old man's mind. He does not mean to be evil, but he comes from a different world—a different *time*. He could twist your priest into something—different, strange. He will do it—"

Glamiss was moving and he pulled the girl along with him. "Take me to them," he said, filled with a sudden cold premonition. Turning briefly, he gave orders to his men and then followed the girl into the deepening gloom of the mountain.

Emeric had, with Asa's meager help, carried Lord Ophir—at his instructions—into a room lined with bays and racks of equipment. Row upon row of lighted tabs surrounded the two dull-metal pedestal tables that rose from the insulated floor. Above the tables, two slabs of the same metal hung from the low ceiling, creating the grisly impression that this was some strange press.

The old man's voice was very thin. Death was stalking him, the Navigator thought. Death was coming to steal the millennia of history that lay compressed in the cells of the ancient brain.

Ophir said, "Place me on the far table."

Emeric did as he was bidden, glad to be free of the frail weight and the musty smell of encroaching death.

"What is this place?" he asked.

"Not now . . . don't question now. You will know . . . everything."

Emeric felt a surging thrill of—what? Intellectual hunger, perhaps. His swift and probing mind was constricted by the age. Was this moment, this old man, and this machine the construct of chance or destiny? he wondered. Could they set him free of feudalism, superstition, and barbarism? He murmured an Ave Stella, praying to God that he was doing His work, and not that of the Adversaries.

But do it he must, he knew with every fiber of his being.

"On the console facing the doorway," the old man whispered. "A control . . . marked *Power*. Press the stud . . ."

Emeric did as he was told, almost brushing Asa aside in his anxiousness to activate this magical work of ancient man's hand. The room began to hum with a soft insistence. The air smelled of thunderstorms.

The Warlock rasped through the countdown. "Activate the bar marked *Auto-time sequence* . . . set the red numbers for your body-mass . . . engage the studs that should be winking yellow now . . . *hurry, priest* . . . there isn't much time. . . ."

Emeric, starship trained, followed the old man's instructions swiftly.

"Priest . . . there will be a visible aura . . . for some hours . . . after the transfer. Don't be afraid . . ." He showed his yellowed teeth in a terrible, sick parody of a smile. "It . . . will impress . . . your savages . . . with your holiness. . . ." He wheezed heavily, his breath coming harder with the effort of speech. "Now . . . set the timer code—the clock face . . . above my head . . . to six. No more than that . . . too much knowledge is a bad thing . . ." Again that skull-smile. *"Is it done?"*

"Yes."

"Tell that—*thing* with you . . . to get out. It could be . . . dangerous to him . . . it . . . whatever. Out . . . *now*."

Emeric signaled Asa out of the humming room. He wondered what the Vulk made of all this. He had said nothing at all, but then, that was the Vulkish way.

"Now," the Warlock said thinly, "lie on the table next

to mine and wait for the timer to take control of the transfer. . . ."

Emeric removed his cowl and mailed shirt and reclined on the dull metal surface. It was strangely warm to the touch. He could hear the old man's rasping breathing over the humming of the air. The smell of thunderstorms grew stronger and the sound rose in pitch. He felt a rapidly increasing stiffness in his limbs, and his vision seemed to grow dimmer.

A sudden leaping panic clutched at him. *Great Star, what had he done to himself?* What dreadful thing had he brought upon himself in his greed for *knowing*?

He would have rolled from the table to the floor, but he was too weak, seemingly, to move the weight of his body. It was as though his muscles had grown *old*.

Beside him he could hear a deeper breathing from Ophir. It was as though his own youth were being drained out of him, being poured into the ancient body of the Warlock.

In terror, Emeric began to pray to the Star, to the Spirit of the Universe.

"Don't—fear," Ophir said. His voice was much stronger, *younger*.

"*What are you doing to me?*" The Navigator did not recognize his own voice. He raised his hand and stared at it. His flesh was glowing with a blue-green fire, cold, insubstantial, ghostly.

Ophir said steadily, "There is a transference both ways, in the beginning. Great God, I haven't felt this strong since—" he laughed with a wild delight—"since when? How can a man count the years I have been drugged, and old?"

Emeric felt his sight deteriorating. Darkness flickered at his eyes, like a bat. "You've tricked me," he gasped feebly. "You are sucking my life out!"

Now, in almost total blackness, he could hear the Warlock's voice. "I wish I could, sir priest! If it were possible, I wouldn't spare you. But the transference is only temporary—that is true and you must believe it—you can't accept a personality imprint if you block it with panic, you fool! Don't fight me . . . *now!*"

The voice was young and powerful, but suddenly Emeric

was unaware of it. It had become unimportant, as unimportant as the clamor he could faintly hear outside the room. Glamiss's voice shouting? Asa saying something? It didn't matter—*nothing* mattered—

A passageway between his mind and that of Lord Ophir ben Rigell ibn Sol alt Messier was opening. A dark vein first, but swiftly widening to contain more and more memories, sights, sounds. He knew instantly the sight of the night sky of Nyor, the sound of ancient music, the feel of Dihanna alt Aldrin's lovemaking, the majesty of his uncle's appearance on the Star Throne, the familiar (to them both, it seemed) tang of Rhada's northern seacoasts—

Then, as suddenly as the opening had appeared, it began to contract, pulsate with jagged impressions: some terrible, some terrible in their pleasure, some indescribable to a brain not addicted to trilaudid—

Emeric's mind, unprepared by anything in his life as simple starship priest and warrior, tottered as he looked into the dark jaws of hell: the shared mind of a drug-addicted paranoid.

The Navigator's scream was shocking in the small room, and it did not stop, but went on and on as Ophir's sophisticated madness slashed daintily at his sanity.

The sight that met Glamiss's eyes as he entered the Personality Exchange Therapy Room both frightened and infuriated him. Shana's warning, and the spectacle of his closest friend writhing in seeming agony on the gray metal slab jolted him into action. Had the apparent victim been someone other than Emeric, the ghostly glow that covered his figure and that of the old Warlock would have stopped him. But the sound of Emeric's animal cries was in his ears, piercing his caution like a sharp quarrel piercing armor to the flesh underneath.

He reacted. Thrusting both Vulk Asa and the girl aside, he bolted toward the Navigator. The machines meant nothing to Glamiss. In fact they resembled nothing more in his experience than the devices found in the deepest parts of Ulm's keeps and used for torture.

The warning shout from Asa was ignored; Glamiss could think only of removing his friend from the torturing slab. His hands closed on Emeric's arm and Shana screamed in terror.

The Navigator's writhings stopped as the fields of the device spread from his nervous system into the axons and dendrites of this new body.

Glamiss seemed frozen, lying half across the slab, his hands welded to his friend's arm by some invisible power. Swiftly, the ghostly blue Saint Elmo's fire spread over him until he seemed to be blazing with cold, flickering flames.

Shana screamed again and sank to her knees, sobbing with superstitious fear. But Vulk Asa, more aware than the human girl of what was happening, began the mental disciplines that would prepare him to intervene if the life-force in the Navigator and warman began to shatter under the pressure of the electronically induced form of Triad.

For the three minds were tightly linked, now. The Vulk could sense the agony of it pulsing through the humming air. Three lives, wildly dissimilar, were being neurologically interwoven. It was a crude process compared to the Triad induced by the Vulkish mind-link, and dangerous. It would have been risky under any circumstances, but the melding of two modern personalities with a third, which was the product of a distant and highly sophisticated age, held the peril of brain-damage and insanity and possibly even physical injury to the nervous system of the three suffering creatures on the gray slabs.

Still, the Vulkish dictum applied: *Do not interfere.* Asa wondered if he could, in fact, stand by and watch Emeric and Glamiss being reduced to human vegetables without intervening. They were, after all, the only humans who had treated him with consideration in the last thousand years of his life—

The Lord Ophir's life-thread was flickering. The temporary infusion of youthful neural vitality was burning up his deteriorated nervous system. He did not care. He seemed apart from the withering old body on the slab of the exchanger. Like a glow-globe near the end of its functioning life, the mind of Ophir ben Rigell burned brightly, the heat of advancing death searing away the drug-damaged blocks in his personality.

Memories and fresh new impressions blazed. He remembered *everything.*

Childhood: the Rhadan sea, silvery under the stormy polar

winds—his father, the brother of the Galacton, saying many times, "Ophir, you will probably have the Star Throne one day and the Feathered Cape and Flail of Empire, so learn to serve, my son—the Imperium is not a thousand suns, it is the people, the human billions who have populated the galaxy —history is the key to all things, the bedrock of all human knowledge, for without a history a race is no better than the beasts of the fields or the fishes of the sea—"

The days, hours, minutes of his life flamed in his surging thoughts. He relived the rearing of a prince—a prince destined to rule a galaxy. *History, yes. And science. And the arts—the gentle arts of music—Dihanna, Dihanna, he thought, I re-member you clearly now!—and painting and sculpture— There was once a man called Michelangelo and another called Steinberg who moved him deeply—and the less gentle arts of war—*

Now, as he remembered the falling suns, the laser-beams with which the Empire could implode a star, he felt the hungry presence of another mind, a soldier's mind, avid to drain him of his knowledge of destruction. Then came to him memories not his own. *The feel of a war mare's warm body between his thighs, the thrill of the charge, the jolting bite of steel into flesh, the sweaty fear of waiting in a darkened starship hold for the opening of the assault valve and then the surge into alien sunlight and the shrieks of men in battle. And something more from this mind, the essence that was Glamiss the War-leader—Ambition, the ravening goad of a desire to conquer, to unite, to dominate. It was purest atavism, the aggressive fury that had been bred out of the ruling class of Rigellian times. It was similar to the anger of the Rimworld barbarians who had swept back into the galactic center to smash the Em-pire, and yet different—for once again it was an outward thrust—a need to bring all the scattered, broken worlds together into—what?* Ophir felt a shuddering thrill in the presence of a terrifying appetite for community. His sophisticated mind recognized it as a crude community of arms and oppression, but it was clearly recognizable for what it was—the Second Empire. As yet unborn, perhaps stillborn if Glamiss died here and now. But Glamiss's mind defied

*death, defied the darkness, dragging Ophir's with it into a
soaring dream of the future—*

Other images, as strong. *A soaring cathedral of steel and
glass beneath a double sun. Algol. Cowled Navigators at their
prayers. The Litanies of Space. Ophir recognized the chanted
words as scientific formulae, the manuals of the ancient starship captains of his own day, committed to memory by these
austere and dedicated priests. I am Emeric Aulus Kiersson-
Rhad, he thought, and felt a flush of pleasure at the Navigator's memories of Rhada's wind-lashed coasts and vast plains.
That, at least, remained the same across the millennia of
Sleep!)*

The interchange of memories was swifter now, as though
this strange Triad sensed that it was burning the life from one
of its members. Ophir, as a gift to the mind of the young
Navigator (he knew now what the Order of Navigators' function was in this time) concentrated on remembering that other
Church that had, in another Dark Time, kept the light of
learning flickering in the night—

Swiftly, and still more swiftly, the memories were shared
among the three. All knew what each knew, their brains burst-
ing with new images.

They saw the galaxy, spinning ponderously in emptiness, a
million parsecs from its nearest neighbor in space. For an instant they struggled with the concept of the Universe's reality,
their merely human minds tottering, reaching, almost grasping—then falling back into the star-glowing spiral that was
Man's present destiny, defeated but exalted.

It was then that death came.

They could feel its lonely cold approaching. Not from the
stars, but from the inner human depths, from the primeval
animal soul of Man. It came out of the molten rock that
cooled into a teeming sea and a chattering tribe in the trees. It
came as the dark leopard, the serpent, the bite of iron, and the
nuclear blast. Not with blinding light, but with shadowed
sadness.

I am dying, brothers. Withdraw, withdraw, Ophir thought.

He sensed the disengagement. It was difficult and painful,
as painful as the birth of their Triad had been. And he sensed

something else, too. For this timeless moment, the Navigator and the Warleader had been one. But now their own personalities began to reassert themselves, and Ophir knew that the soldier was thinking of the power he now held, the knowledge of weapons that lay in the armory within the mountain and what they could mean to a conqueror-to-be. The priest was remembering the hell of war that had brought his Order into being and understanding, for the first time, that primitive men's power to kill one another must be tightly leashed, lest a permanent darkness fall.

But Ophir's nervous system was used up, seared by the flood of youth that had coursed through him under the influence of the machine. His brain alone functioned now, and soon it would stop, for his heart had stopped beating, his blood was cooling.

He made a last effort.

Do not fight one another, brothers, he cautioned. *Work together.*

He sensed the growing dichotomy, the divergent sense of purpose in the two young minds he had primed with his life's knowledge.

He was regretful, but to him it could no longer matter. The primeval darkness closed in on him. He felt—alone. Glamiss and Emeric were gone and, with them, their vitality.

Yet it was strange. Death, that had a moment ago seemed so worrisome, came now as a friend. It is time, Ophir ben Rigell ibn Sol alt Messier thought, mentally smiling at his pompous, man-made dignities. Dihanna, it is time and past time.

The electrical activity in the old brain cells that was Ophir slowed and peacefully stopped.

The Warlock of Rhada was dead.

He had given Emeric and Glamiss a glimpse of the final serene darkness. It was his last gift.

Chapter Seventeen

The moment that Glamiss donned the feathered cape, he laid claim to the Star Throne. Considering that his following was fewer than fifty fighting men, it was a gesture of astonishing arrogance—and courage.
> —Nav (Bishop) Julianus Mullerium, *The Age of the Star Kings*, Middle Second Stellar Empire period

That night on Aldrin, called Vyka by the folk of that place, the Mythic Age died in a single thunderclap, killed by the hand of a Saint. I can say no more.
> —From the Testament of Anselm Styr, Navigator, burned by the Inquisition in the last year of Talvas Hu Chien's Grand Mastership

Glamiss and Emeric went to the valley of Trama-Vyka as strangers and friends. They left it as enemies and brothers.
> —Vikus Bel Cyb-1009, *Rhadan Influences in Galactic History*, Middle Confederate period

Lord Ulm of Vara sat heavily on his war mare and surveyed the scene before him with dull despair. The light fading from the greenish Vykan sky still exposed a vista of military disaster. Five assaults had been launched against the rebellious warmen entrenched on the mountain, and the only tangible result lay all about him in the mounds of dead and the straggling lines of wounded.

Ulm's slow mind struggled with the concept of defeat and what defeat would mean to him personally. Already, Linne Warleader was muttering to the other captains about Ulm's inability to dislodge the rebels from their position. The leaders were listening to him, throwing dark glances at their bondlord.

But that was not the worst. Halfway up the bloodied moraine the Bishop-Navigator was counting the casualties, ordering wounded men out of the action, and back to the starship in the meadow. Kaifa would not do that if he did not despair of Ulm's ever accomplishing what he had set out to do.

In the light of afternoon, how simple it had appeared, Ulm thought dully. This morning he had left his keep with a thousand men and the approval of the Order of Navigators. Now the remains of his force stood near to mutiny and the Bishop offered no help, his dark Arab face grim in the fading light of the Vyka sun.

Ulm's clumsy mind grappled with the reality of his situation. His warmen could be taken from him at any moment by any captain with a solution to the absurd blind alley into which the Varan force had drifted. It seemed to the warlord that Fate was conspiring against him. He had no sense that if Fate had conspired, it was not specifically against *him*, but in favor of another. The nexus of power had formed in this valley. A politico-military nucleus had taken shape, formed by forces stretching across time and distances beyond his imagining.

The forces were not beyond Kaifa's imagining—far from it. The Bishop stood surrounded by more than enough military power to accomplish what the Order had directed him to accomplish. But it had been so badly used that he was helpless now. The fault, he told himself, was his own. From its inception, the move against Glamiss and this valley had been ill-starred. Small mistakes had grown into a pattern of personal catastrophe—*personal*, because the Order *always* survived and prospered. That was the bitterest reality, and—strangely—the only satisfaction the worldly priest could claim. For within that mountain, amid those marvels of Empire science he, Kaifa, had hoped to take for himself and the Order, was another priest. Suddenly, in the declining Vykan day, the power had shifted from his own experienced hands into those of Emeric Kiersson-Rhad.

For the first time in many years, Kaifa of Nasser, Bishop of the Order of Navigators, felt humbled by the strange and mysterious ways of God in the Star.

Linne Warleader marshaled his company for the last assault of the fading day on the rebels entrenched on the mountain. The troopers had lighted torches to make a fire-charge, and the orange light turned the bloodied rocks black. Linne did not imagine that his charge would be successful, but he had weighed the temper of his own men and those led by the other captains, and he felt certain that one more costly repulse would bring general revolt against the authority of the Lord Ulm.

Then, as custom demanded, he would seek the priest's permission (which could not be refused) to challenge Ulm for the holding of Vara. The laws and customs of the feudatories of the Great Sky were simple and direct. A warlord ruled so long as he was fit to rule. Defeat was reason enough to cause his subordinates to challenge him.

The firelight played on Linne's heavily bearded face. His eyes, close-set on either side of the iron nose-piece of his cone-shaped helmet, held an expression of triumph. He would lead the charge, even knowing it could not succeed. Then he would kill Ulm, assume his mantle, and settle down to starve the rebels from the warrens within the mountain. No amount of Empire warlockry could save them then. And the Bishop would return to Algol only after having consecrated Linne as holder of the lands of Vara-Vyka.

For a moment his dark mind even toyed with the idea of holding Kaifa and the *Gloria* on Vyka. A warlord with a starship of his own could spread havoc among the Rimworlds. Linne's ambition, though livelier than the cloddish Ulm's, still extended no farther than that.

The fear of excommunication touched him. Not because he feared the Star: Linne was a godless man—but because the men of Vyka would probably not follow a leader whom the Order refused to consecrate.

But one would see about that—later. Linne turned to give the command for the firecharge . . .

Quite suddenly the rebel position blazed with light.

The men in the moraine stared upward in superstitious fright. The light of their torches faded to insignificance in the incandescent glow from above. The war mares cried out their fear and anger.

Ulm's face grew pale under his grimy beard. The Bishop, too, stared upward. He, of all those below, came nearest to understanding that the blaze of light was not supernatural, but some manifestation of Empire science. Yet it struck dismay into his heart.

Linne, his useless torch still held in his left hand, his heavy sword in his right, gaped at the gorgeous apparition that had materialized on the platform by the tunnel mouth.

Glamiss stood in a feathered cape that scintillated with a glory of light and color no Vykan had ever seen before. Yet it touched a hundred hidden strands of racial memory.

The young warrior stood draped in the regalia of the ancient King-Elector, heir to the Star Throne of a thousand suns.

A hushed murmuring fell on the armed men. Glamiss, his trappings sending spears of color and light into the darkening night, raised his arms. His voice, strangely amplified, rang out over the valley of Trama. Even the Navigators in the grounded starship a kilometer away heard it clearly.

"People of Vyka! Hear me!"

The warmen of Ulm's levy had never before been addressed as the "people" of anywhere. They were bonded warmen, predators to be sure, but little better than slaves in the service of a lord of a dark land. They listened, half-afraid, half-moved, as Glamiss spoke to them.

"You know me, Vykans! There is not one of you who does

not know me! Now listen to what I have to say to you—"

Kaifa, dazzled by the vision of a young Star King, stared open-mouthed. Years ago he had seen painted images of the great imperials, the kings of Nyor. This Vykan, this *barbarian*, was wearing the regalia of the Rigellian Galactons! A storm of conflicting emotions shook the Navigator's sanity. The very look of the Vykan challenged ancestral loyalties even as it outraged priestly reverence for the ancient past.

Glamiss said clearly, "Here in the mountain is what is left of the Empire." He raised his hand to display a small, rounded cone. "I command its powers!"

From the cone a thin beam of ruby light materialized as if by magic. Glamiss played it along the moraine and the rocks bubbled, coruscated, and ran molten.

"I command this weapon—*and many more like it.*"

The mares shrieked and backed away from the red-glowing stream of melted stone that trickled down the moraine. Kaifa bit his lips until he tasted blood. *A laser pistol.* No such weapon had been fired or even found in the known galaxy for four thousand years or more. Great Star, what else must there be in that mountain? he wondered.

Glamiss spoke again as the laser-beam flickered and died. "Within the heart of the mountain is a Falling Sun." He searched the sea of upward-turned faces. "Do you understand me? Do you understand what it is in my power to do?"

Kaifa could stand no more. He thrust back his cowl and screamed, *"Blasphemy! The Adversaries speak!"*

Glamiss's eyes searched out the Bishop. Kaifa shivered. Even at this distance he could see that some Power did, indeed, speak with Glamiss of Vyka's voice. The face was that of a young man, but the *eyes*—the eyes were filled with a knowledge of things a man of this barbarian time could only imagine. Kaifa felt crushed and humbled by the weight of that knowledge.

"Hear me, Vykans," Glamiss said more gently, though his voice still rang out over the dark valley. "It was Destiny that brought us to this place. Not the Adversaries, warmen, but the veritable Spirit of the Star." His tone grew strangely distant. "If only I could share with you what I have learned, good

people. If only it were possible. I have seen the glorious past of
our race. I have seen a thousand suns shining on one flag, one
people. *And it will be so again!*"

The warmen, sensing that something unique was happening,
something huge and sky-moving, waited, listening.

"It begins here," Glamiss said. "I raised the flag here—
and—it—ends—*in Nyor*!"

The warmen stirred and stared at one another at the mention of fabled Nyor—the El Dorado, the capital of the
Universe where gold and gems lay in the street for the taking.
Was he offering them Nyor, they wondered? It was as though
some savage king of another age offered men Valhalla—while
they yet lived.

Glamiss's voice turned harsh and demanding. "Ulm! Where
are you, Ulm?" He searched the gathering and found his
quondam lord. "You named me rebel, Ulm! You brought
these men against me! Now I challenge you for Vara!"

Ulm stared at the cone-weapon still in Glamiss's hand, his
eyes round and protuberant, the sweat bathing his hairy
cheeks.

Glamiss moved down the rubbled moraine and the blaze of
light flamed about him, streaming from the stuff of the
feathered cape woven for an Emperor's heir. "Answer my
challenge, Ulm! Do it now. Because these men of Vara are
mine when this is done. And I will use them to take all of
Vyka, and then Vyka will take the Rim—and the Rim will take
Nyor! So answer my challenge, Ulm!"

"No!" The strangled cry came not from Ulm, but from
Linne, mounted and armed, plunging from the ranks to con-
front Glamiss. *"No, by all the Stars, it shall not be!"*

He spurred at Glamiss, sword swinging free. From above
came a cry of alarm: the folk of Trama had gathered there to
watch the frightening play of events.

Kaifa waited for Glamiss to burn down the charging Linne
with the laser, and then realized that instead, the younger man
had drawn his flail.

Linne's mare galloped swiftly, her claws bared, lips drawn
back in a battle-shriek. Linne struck with his heavy-bladed
weapon, and Glamiss's morningstars screamed across the cut-

ting edge as Linne went past, whirled his mare, and charged again.

The tip of the sword pierced Glamiss's mail and sent a feather of light from the glorious cape drifting into the darkness beyond the blaze of illumination in which they fought.

Linne yelled savagely and whirled still again, but as he charged this time, Glamiss's flail caught his wrist and jerked him from his mare's back. He tore himself free and struggled upright, grasping his sword with both hands. His face was distorted into a grimace of rage and frustration. He charged again on foot, stumbling in his manic fury against the upstart who would steal Vara from him.

He saw only the swift flashing of the starred iron as it descended on his face, and that was the last he ever knew, for the flail crushed him.

The warmen of Vara beat their weapons together in approval. They had been frightened by the manifestations they had seen, but this was a thing they knew and understood. A man had won their loyalty in single combat.

Glamiss turned to look up at the folk gathered on the platform above. He could see that Emeric had appeared among them. Emeric, his brother—more closely related to him now than any other man could ever be, for they had shared the Warlock of Rhada's memories, and his death.

He heard the suddenly shouted warning and turned to see old Ulm, his face white and desperate, riding him down. There was a whirring and a sullen thud, and the lord of Vara's face went blank with surprise.

He galloped past, tottering, clutching his saddlehorn, to fall among the darkened stones. There he lay still, the depressed wound of a crossbow quarrel welling blood.

Behind him, standing among the warmen, Bishop Kaifa held the crossbow.

Glamiss moved down the moraine and the warmen gathered about him, acknowledging his overlordship now easily, for there remained no one to challenge him for it.

When he reached the Bishop, Glamiss said, "Why? You saved my life—why?"

The Bishop's thin, dark face seemed hewn from old iron.

"The mountain. You *know* what it is, you know everything about it—"

"Not everything," Glamiss said, remembering the dead Warlock. "But enough."

Kaifa's eyes glittered. "What is hidden there can bring us back to where we were—when the suns fell."

Glamiss turned thoughtfully to look up to the place where Emeric stood. "Yes," he said. "To that same place."

Emeric said, "And now it begins, the jihad, the holy war?"

They stood alone in the library, a room they understood much better now, fortified as they were with the dead Ophir's memories.

Glamiss remained silent for a long time. "Is there another way, Nav?" he asked at last.

The priest did not reply. They had both been touched with the bitter wisdom that comes with age during their time under the Personality Exchanger. It would not do for them to lie to one another.

Glamiss smiled mirthlessly, his mind fixed on the long bleak road ahead. "We are not Vulk, after all," he said.

Emeric nodded, "We go alone, then."

Glamiss spoke earnestly. "Not alone, Emeric. Together, you and I." He smiled again, a shadow of the carefree warrior's grin Emeric remembered. "All the way to Nyor."

"Where the streets are paved with gold?"

"And the women are all beautiful."

The Navigator shook his head. "No, my friend. We don't go together."

Glamiss frowned. "Why not? I have Vara. I'll soon have Vyka. Then the Rimworlds—"

"I know—the jihad to make a new Galacton."

Glamiss's eyes turned hard. "Is that wrong?"

"I don't know," the priest said heavily. "It's human."

"A few years—no more, Emeric—"

The Navigator shook his head. "A lifetime, Glamiss. Maybe more."

The warman laughed. "Not so, friend priest. With the weapons stored here—the knowledge we'll take from this place—"

"The Falling Suns? Atomics?"

"Only if necessary," Glamiss said, frowning.

"No, Glamiss. Not that way."

Glamiss stared at him from under lowering brows. *He's already becoming a king,* Emeric thought. *He has the arrogance of power growing in him. How strange it was that each of us took from the old Warlock what was most natural to our makeup. Glamiss the glory and arrogance, I the self-doubts and the fears—*

"Glamiss," Emeric said sadly, "you have Vara, as you say. It is a small holding, but it gives you a base of power. And you'll have all of Vyka very soon, I have no doubt. I don't know how many men will die across the Great Sky before you found your Second Empire—" He smiled ruefully. "Remember your dream of Nyor? You have the feathered cape—you'll have the golden city, too, I have no doubt. You'll find the streets aren't paved with gold, but that won't matter in the end. You will have the Queen of the Skies—" He turned away and made the sign of the Star on his breast, filled with a sadness he could not contain. "I wish I could believe it is right, old friend. I wish I could be so certain—"

"What are you saying to me?" Glamiss demanded.

Emeric felt the stab of his own disloyalty. He wondered how many years would pass before the bitterness of this moment died away for them both. He said, "What will be, will be. It is the will of God." His blue Rhadan eyes turned steely. *"But there will be no magic weapons, Glamiss. No lasers, no killing of men from far away. You will fight—but by all the Stars, you'll see the men you kill up close and know that you are paying a terrible price for Nyor."*

Glamiss's hands closed vise-like on the Navigator's shoulders as the Vykan guessed at what thing Emeric had done.

Emeric nodded slowly. "You begin to understand me, Glamiss Conqueror. That's good. I've pulled the cadmium rods from the nuclear pile below and destroyed them. There is nothing you can do. We have—" he glanced at the ancient chronometer on the wall—"about forty minutes before the pile goes critical and sends this mountain into the sky." He ignored the pain of Glamiss's tightening grip that pressed the iron mail of his shirt into his flesh. "We can move everyone into the *Gloria* and escape—or we can stay here and be part of the last nuclear blast of the Dark Time. The choice is yours, Glamiss Warleader.''

For a moment the Navigator thought Glamiss might kill him; his thin face grew livid and the eyes seemed to turn black with rage.

"Do you know what you've done?" Never had he heard such hatred in a voice.

Emeric said, ''Yes, I know what I've done.''

Glamiss stepped back and stood for a moment, his hands white-knuckled on his weapons. His voice was strangled with fury, and as cold as the death of friendship. ''When we reach Vara, I want you gone. Never let me see your face again— *brother*.''

He turned and swept from the room, already regal in his movements, Emeric thought ruefully.

Was I right? he asked himself. *Did I have the right to destroy all this knowledge? Knowing nothing could be preserved save a few trivial things, would I do it again?*

Yes. *Yes*, by all that men held holy—he *would* do it again. And again. And still again. Better that Glamiss spend his life at war killing thousands than he have the science of the past to spend months killing billions. Because no Empire, no matter how necessary, could ever be built by men without war and killing. We are still too near to our australopithecine ancestors for that, the priest thought firmly.

He glanced at the chronometer and heard the growing confusion of retreat and withdrawal in the corridors of the hospital. He looked about longingly at the library and then forced himself to gather his thoughts. It was time to go.

The *Gloria in Coelis* was near the boundary of space when the valley of Trama vanished in fire. The mushroom pillar glowed crimson, yellow, vermilion, and white in the darkness of Vyka's night.

The novices at the control consoles stared through the tinted shields, muttering Aves and crossing themselves with the sign of the Star.

Bishop Kaifa, his face drawn and yellowish with anger, spoke in a voice that rasped like steel on glass. ''You are either a saint or a madman, Nav Emeric. It will be the duty of the Grand Master to decide which. Now get out of my sight and stay out; I can't bear to look at you."

Emeric made his genuflection to his superior and left the bridge. He was thinking that Talvas Hu Chien was a priest of the severe persuasion, a book burner—a killer of scientists. Ironically, the old Grand Master's savagery would probably approve of what Emeric had done.

Emeric made his way toward his own quarters. The starship was crowded with the levy of Vara, the folk of Trama (dispossessed now, because of what Emeric had done—their beautiful valley a radiating, boiling ruin), and even the Tramans' livestock.

"Nav—Lord."

Emeric looked down into Shana's pinched, dark face. He had forgotten about the girl. Was she mourning her eagles? he wondered. He had destroyed them, too.

"What will become of us, Lord?"

What could he say that would have any meaning to her? "You will be given new land—somewhere else, Shana."

"Our valley is gone?"

He nodded slowly.

"Who did this wicked thing to us?"

Who, indeed? "I did, Shana."

The girl studied him intently. Since his experience on the Personality Exchanger there had been a difference in the way she treated him—a strange, touching diffidence that was unlike her.

"Was it necessary, Lord?"

Emeric's face grew stern. "Yes. It was necessary."

The girl was silent for a time, and Emeric made to move past her. He was tired and sick at heart and longed for the silence and emptiness of his cell-like room. But Shana said, "The Lord Glamiss is angry."

"Very," Emeric said dryly.

"He has offered us land, but I wanted to ask you."

"He has the right now, Shana. Vara-Vyka is his."

"There is talk among the folk that you are a great lord on a world called Rhada."

"I have lands there," Emeric said.

"That was the Warlock's place."

"He was born there," Emeric said, remembering. The rest of it couldn't be so easily explained to this weyrherd girl. But that the Warlock had been born by the Rhad north sea—that she could understand.

"Will you settle us on your land, Lord?"

"You want to go off-world?"

"Yes. Our valley is fire. There is no place here for us."

Emeric the Rhadan disputed with Emeric the Navigator—but only for a short time. The folk of Trama deserved that much from him, at least. Perhaps, he thought ruefully, they'll found a dynasty of their own one day—when Glamiss Magnifico is ruler of all the Great Sky.

"It will be done, Shana," he said.

And then the girl did a strange thing. She touched the hem of his habit and brought her fingers to her lips. The cult of St. Emeric is born, he thought ironically. The cult of the man who flamed the last mountain into the sky.

He walked on alone now, knowing that he would always be alone, the object of an Emperor-to-be's bitterness.

Was I right? he wondered. He might one day ask the Vulk, but he knew that they would not tell him. They would not tell him until he grew wise enough to know without being told.

He closed himself into his tiny humming cell and knelt at the prie-dieu. How long, he wondered, would he ask himself the thing Shana had asked him, the thing he had answered with such certainty?

He spoke aloud, forehead pressed against the thrumming metal.

"Was it necessary, Lord?"

And as the starship drifted slowly across the line that divided night from day and into the light of the Vyka sun, Emeric had his answer.